THE ERIK BLAIR DIARIES

Praise for John W. Whitehead and *The Erik Blair Diaries*

"No one but John Whitehead could tell this tale and make it believable. It's a terrifying blueprint made bitingly believable by an unflinching observer of our eroding rights, and a fearless crusader against injustice and corruption. Whitehead is the ferocious watchdog of government corruption and abuse of power in this country and a stinging gadfly about the flagrant disregards of the Constitution. John Whitehead's books have been described as 'science fiction with footnotes,' and in *The Erik Blair Diaries* he injects his expertise and gritty believability into a frighteningly realized future. This is not a Sci Fi fantasy, it's a vividly imagined prediction of a nightmare that will happen. It's a heart-stopping, un-put-downable headlong rush." — David Dalton, *New York Times* bestselling author and a founding editor of *Rolling Stone*

"John Whitehead is an indefatigable warrior for truth and justice that I have admired for many years. Here he lays out a stark reminder of the world we are heading into so fast unless sanity, courage and self-respect prevail – NOW." — David Icke, best-selling author of *The Biggest Secret*

"John Whitehead is not only one of the nation's most consistent and persistent civil libertarians. He is also a remarkably perceptive illustrator of our popular culture, its insights and dangers. I often believe that John Whitehead is channeling the principles of James Madison, who would be very proud of him." — Nat Hentoff, nationally syndicated columnist

"The loss of personal liberty, the growth of big government, and the death of government respect for persons rarely occur overnight. It takes a fine eye and a fearless manner to discover and reveal these dangers before it is too late. No one in America today does this better than John

Whitehead." — Hon. Andrew P. Napolitano, Senior Judicial Analyst, Fox News Channel, Distinguished Visiting Professor of Law, Brooklyn Law School

"John Whitehead is one of the most eloquent and knowledgeable defenders of liberty, and opponents of the growing American police state, writing today." — Ron Paul, 12-term US Congressman and former Presidential candidate

THE ERIK BLAIR DIARIES

BATTLEFIELD OF THE DEAD

JOHN W. WHITEHEAD

Waterside Productions

Cover illustration by Adam Archer
Cover design by Christopher Combs

Printed in the United States of America

First Printing, 2021

ISBN-13: 978-1-954968-02-8 print edition
ISBN-13: 978-1-954968-03-5 ebook edition

Waterside Productions
2055 Oxford Ave
Cardiff, CA 92007
www.waterside.com

For Nisha

TABLE OF CONTENTS

CHAPTER 1
THE CONTRABAND

"Stop. Step to the street and drop your contraband."—Robofly

I could never forget that face.

That haggard, worn face.

I could never forget those eyes.

Eyes filled with horror, awe and some other emotion I couldn't quite place.

He seemed to know me. Yet I had never seen him before in my life.

Still, I will never forget his words.

They exploded from his parched lips like a detonated bomb. "It's here. It's all true!" he cried, falling to his knees before me on the crowded pavement.

He held one hand up towards the brown-hazed sky. "God help us! God..." Spittle dripped off his chin.

I couldn't look away.

He was looking at me now, imploringly, searchingly, pinning me in place. I stepped back, years of training urging me to disengage, look away, and not meddle in what doesn't concern me.

Still...

Before I could act, he grabbed my pant leg. "This is for you," he rasped as he pushed a tattered, rectangular package at me. "Quick. Take it! Guard it! It is your future and my past. It is your destiny. It is—"

As quickly as he'd appeared in my life, the broken man collapsed on the crowded sidewalk. His eyes rolled back into his skull. His eyelids closed. He crumbled face-forward onto the pavement. And then he was gone.

The tattered, brown package tumbled to the ground, landing like a descending gliderbot. The brilliance of the flashing urban lights illuminated the backside of the man's corpse splayed on the pavement. His torn coat spread like wings on both sides of his body.

The crowded sidewalk was hot, so hot it was difficult to breathe. It was filled with humans who never broke stride, staring straight ahead, zombie-like, lest they arouse suspicion. Some stepped over the dead man's body as if he were a piece of mislaid rubbish or a pile of dog feces.

Then I heard the all-too-familiar whirring, buzzing sound resonating over the crowded streets.

I hate that noise.

It was those cursed roboflies.

They were coming.

The sensors in the sidewalks had probably alerted the roboflies to the corpse. Or was it the ever-present, ubiquitous surveillance devices?

Either way, nothing escaped their senses or their view.

I had only a moment, if that.

I moved quickly.

Dropping to one knee next to the body, I placed my fingertips on his wrist to confirm what I already knew. No pulse.

From the corner of my eye, I could see the parcel.

"This is for you. Quick. Take it! Guard it! It is your future and my past. It is your destiny." What could he have meant? Surely he had mistaken me for someone else?

Still, driven by a strange impulse I didn't quite understand, blotting out the warning siren in my head over what was surely a forbidden act, I snatched the slender package from the sidewalk, tucking it inside my coat.

Hopefully, the surveillance cameras hadn't gleaned my subterfuge.

Standing up, I joined the crowded citizens marching in lockstep down the sidewalks, eyes plastered straight ahead, never looking to the side, never looking up, never making eye contact with anyone—or anything—lest I draw the ire of one of those buzzing fiends.

"Stand aside. Stand aside! Now! Move away from the body," a robotic voice ordered from behind me.

"Human down, stand aside," another robotic voice droned.

A laser bolt smashed the concrete. Human shrieks filled the murky haze.

The crowd scattered, leaving an opening around the supine body.

I knew better than to look over my shoulder or make any type of out-of-sync movement separate and apart from the teeming crowd. My last run-in with a robofly the year before had resulted in severe burns on the back of my neck. I've still got the scars, a reminder that absolute obedience is the only kind of freedom granted to us.

Up ahead, I could see the street corner where I would make my turn.

Rounding the corner, I slid between passersby without any sudden movements that would set me apart from the throng. Only another block and a half to go.

Overhead, the roboflies were scanning the crowds for nonconforming movements, hidden weapons or anything that could possibly hint at concealed contraband.

Those bastard bugs were everywhere!

Thankfully, my contraband seemed to blend in among the sea of purses, backpacks, and P2Ps.

"Stop. Step to the street and drop your contraband!" a shrill robotic voice commanded.

I stopped, stomach acid rushing upward, bile filling the back of my throat.

"It's him!" a woman screamed. A young man raced past me, darting straight through the crowd, looking hurriedly over his shoulder.

"Atlas Four! Atlas Four! Suspect headed your way!" one of the little metallic insects alerted. The android cops that patrolled the streets quickly closed in on the suspect, moving toward him in concentric circles.

He was a goner.

With a resigned sigh of relief, I moved on. There was nothing I could do about him. I had my own hide to worry about.

For the moment, at least, I was safe.

I was finally home.

I entered my building and hurried down the dingy, dirty hallway toward the elevator.

"Blair, Erik," I announced to the voice analyzer.

"Enter," the voice analyzer ordered.

Striding into the empty, waiting elevator, I adopted a blank stare for the always watching screens as the cube began the upward climb.

Moments later, the doors slid open.

"Thirteenth Floor, exit to your left."

Stopping at the door marked B-71446, I opened my eyes wide and stared straight ahead.

"Iris scan complete. Enter," commanded the voice on the scanner that sits eye-level on the door. Always the same mantra every night.

With a click, the door opened.

With another soft click, the door automatically closed behind me. Locking me in and the world out.

"Room temperature 72 Fahrenheit," the smartmeter intoned. "No other humanoids present," it matter-of-factly stated, a niggling reminder that we are constantly being scanned, identified, and added to the government's central database.

Our whereabouts are continually monitored.

We are data.

The adrenaline that had kicked in on the street was giving way to a hunger to know more about the package tucked under my outerwear.

How many times had I been drilled in school about the dangers of curiosity? Yet here I was, desperate to know what was in the purloined package.

My P2P, sitting on my night table and digitally connected to the tiny, almost undetectable surveillance cameras situated on the ceiling and at every corner of the room, buzzed and lit up. Focused on my face, it alerted me to the fact that government eyes knew I had returned. My every movement was being scrutinized.

I would have to proceed cautiously.

Sitting on the edge of the bed, I unsnapped the clasp on one shoe, then the other, and placed them both on the floor. Tucking my pillow up behind me, I sat on the bed, my P2P in my lap. I placed the contraband on top of my P2P, thus blocking the screen, and settled in with the rancid looking package.

Tied around the slender rectangle rather neatly was a thin cloth string. I unbound it, laying the thread on the night table.

Leaning back on my pillow, I ran my hand over the surface of the strange object. Running my fingers beneath the flap, I opened the package to reveal a thick stack of neatly folded, tattered pages.

I thumbed through the lightly browned pages with their peculiar, musty smell.

I'd never seen anything like it before, but I'd heard about it.

This was paper, the stuff of yesteryear, the basis of books and newspapers and libraries, before the world went digital and P2Ps and screen devices took over.

Unfolding the pages, I was immediately drawn into the words.

The strange words, oddly scrambled on the paper yet fixed in time and space in a way no P2P could manage, jumped out at me. My eyes were fixated, my mind awhirl.

I read silently.

I read slowly.

CHAPTER 2
THE WEREWOLVES

"I think, therefore I am—I am a criminal."—Words from the Contraband

Here I am again.
Back in the empty room. This strange empty room.
Nothing in it but space and silence.
A tomb for the yet living.
Unquestionably, it means death.
My eyes scan the ceiling. No light anywhere, except for that filtered down into my eyes from the dim, purple light.
But why death? Death? I've never feared death.
Even in my dreams I've always realized where I was at.
But I've finally arrived at death's door.
I'm here.
I know it.

Strange, fascinating words.
I read on, my lips silently tracing each word.

The drugs, the effects of the monster drugs are beginning to wear off.
Did I talk? Did I confess?
What did I tell the Werewolves? The evil Werewolves!
God, my skin hurts.

I dare not crawl over and peer into the blood-splattered sink. Blood
I coughed up out of my dying lungs.
I'm talking to myself again.
I'm writing to no one from nowhere.
If, by chance, someone from somewhere should read these words,
mark what I say and run for your life.
Or should I say, run to your death.
That's where we are all headed anyway, we of the faceless throngs.
Our programs are predetermined to cease operation. Our DNA is
manipulated to make sure we don't last too long. Just long enough
to not cause too much trouble.
I have overstayed my welcome. I have caused just enough trouble
to make death worthwhile. I will not die a slave to the beast.
Please hear me! You've been lied to. Trust no one. Not even yourself.
You've been programmed to believe that lies are truth. Your life is
a lie. Your existence is a lie. Your reality is a lie. Only death is real.
Only love is true.

Programs, predetermined existence and the Werewolves.
This was heresy: the words that had been written.
This was treason: dangerous ideas now consumed.
My mind was a muddled mess.
I had to stop.
Think.
I couldn't help myself.
I could not stop reading.

It's all about mind control. They bombard our heads with elec-
trorays and alter our thought patterns. They reconfigure our reali-
ties and hardwire our dreams.
They call themselves the government of the people. But they do not
govern. They rule. They may walk as men, but they feed on our
carcasses like monsters.

Yes, this was treason.

Treason for the eyes to look upon it, treason for the mind to comprehend, treason for the heart to agree with it as surely as the words resonated deep within me.

It was as if the author and I shared one mind: here were all the secret, furtive thoughts I had scarcely dared to think, let alone utter, for fear of running afoul of the Thought Police.

I read on.

Think, people! Ideas are more powerful than guns. They cannot risk a population of thinkers. Thinkers become doers. That way lies resistance! The Controllers are powerful only so long as they can intimidate and terrify and coerce the people to cower like mice, but they cannot prevail against people who think for themselves.

There is power in numbers. The people have forgotten that, but it is their secret weapon and the only path to freedom.

The Butcher reigns over the slaughterhouse. It is his playground. It is his bloody palette. But he has no true power. All he knows is how to chop and skewer and kill. He is merely the meat grinder for the Controllers.

To stop the slaughter, the people must cease to be lambs. They must awaken. They must resist. They must refuse to go meekly to their own deaths.

My hands were trembling now. My throat was on fire. My eyes stung. This was no stranger. Of that I was convinced.

But how? And why? And what was I to do now?

I read on.

I have become a criminal. For your sake, as well as my own. If you're reading my crimes now—and God, I hope you are—then I have not suffered in vain. What are my crimes? I think, therefore I am—I am a criminal.

You understand that much, at least, but soon you will understand more.

With enlightenment comes pain. I wish I could spare you the pain, but there can be no escape from this hellish prison without it.

This diary is my last will and testament. It is a map to help you navigate the terrain that awaits you. But be warned: the evil ones have no mercy.

Sweat was dotting my forehead and my breathing was labored. I had a bad feeling this was not going to end well for me or the mysterious writer.

The drugs are tearing me apart.

My hair has started falling out. My skin has turned the purple of a dying day. Oh God, my skin has started peeling off in places.

My throat has reversed its function. Nothing will stay down.

No food. No drink.

Only blood seems to drain down and then up and out of my retching throat.

All this in a society that can treat virtually any disease.

No matter. As long as I can feel the pain, I still live. I must live a little longer. Just long enough to—

"Violation! Violation!" My P2P began screaming out its alert.

That little fiend had alerted the central database concerning the contraband. Now the walls were screaming accusations at me in surround sound.

I was in trouble.

Big trouble.

I should have known the P2P would access my visuals of the contraband via the temporal lobe chip embedded in my head.

What an idiot I am!

Grabbing the contraband, I snatched up my shoes in one hand and ran for the door, slamming it open with a crash.

Darting into the hallway, it hit me: the elevator would not admit me now.

I was a suspect, a criminal.

An Atlas Four or maybe more hideous androids were on their way. At the least, they would be waiting for me downstairs.

"Erik, come this way," a harried but soft voice called out.

Turning, I saw an angel in rags, beauty in disarray.

"Come. You only have a few seconds."

I ran towards her, still clutching my precious bundle.

"Wait," she said as she placed a small, bullet-shaped object on my forehead. "This will neutralize your lobe chip. You're no longer trackable, for now at least."

"Who are you?" I gasped.

"No time for that," she said as she grabbed my hand and hurried me down the hallway to a door marked "Exit." Again, ripping the bullet-shaped object from her shirt pocket, the girl waved it over the security screen and the door burst open.

"What is that thing?" I asked, amazed.

"It's a magic bullet," she replied. "Let's go."

Running, she led me down a flight of stairs and through another door. We were now on the floor beneath mine. Stepping into a small, closeted area littered with plastic trash bags, she whispered, "We can hide here for a while until the initial alert dies down."

Her eyes lingered on the bundle in my hand before scrutinizing my face with a quizzical stare.

CHAPTER 3
EILEEN

"I'm your Watcher."—Eileen

How to explain the contraband when I didn't understand it myself? I tucked the packet under my arm and away from her curious gaze.

Frankly, I had a few questions of my own: Who was she? What did she want? How did she happen to show up at the very moment I was fleeing trouble? How did she know my name? And why was she putting herself in jeopardy to help me?

I started to say something, but all I got was a "shhh" from my closetmate.

"Don't do or say anything to alert the sensors to our presence," she said. Placing her back against the wall, she gradually slid to the floor.

I kneeled and then sat down facing her, folding my knees in front of me, my back against the opposite wall. It was dark except for the light peeking under the door.

She sat there for several minutes looking intently at me, studying my dimly lit face. I did the same to her. Her long black hair lay partially draped across her right shoulder. She was pretty, but not like the girls I knew at the Academy who were always getting something sculpted or touched up. She looked like someone who was comfortable in her own skin.

"Here," she said quietly, handing me a small red pill. "Take this. It will temporarily slow your heartrate and alter your body temp. We need to throw off the kinetic scanners."

She placed a pill on her tongue. After a moment's hesitation, I echoed her movements. The pill tasted like candy and dissolved quickly in my mouth.

I watched as her eyes closed and her head slumped to the side.

I was feeling drowsy as well. I dropped off into blackness.

Then like an explosion, light was all around me.

I was standing on something high. A narrow ledge. A platform. A foothold of some sort. I couldn't tell if I was standing on a skyscraper looking down on a metropolis or a mountaintop looking down on a valley, but I was so high up that everything beneath me was a gray haze sprinkled throughout with golden sunlight.

I had an overwhelming urge to know what lay beneath me.

Bending forward a bit, I looked down. And in looking down, I began free-falling fast like a descending bomb. My arms were spread wide. I could feel the wind rushing through my hair. The world was rushing past me, but it was a world I didn't know.

For a moment, I lost myself in the sense of weightlessness, in the blur of colors racing past me at supersonic speed.

Then things slowed down for a moment and I saw what I was falling towards, and it was death. I began to struggle, fighting gravity, fighting the momentum that was dragging me downwards, fighting to hold onto the few shreds of life I had left and resist what waited for me with gaping jaws and jagged teeth.

Just as I was about to crash land my way into oblivion, I felt something tug at my arm and jerk me back.

"Erik, wake up!" The tugging continued.

I opened my eyes to find I was back in the closet. Back in a world I knew, at least.

My blurred vision began to clear. An anxious face stared down at me.

"How do you know my name?" I asked.

"I know your name because I've been watching you."

"Watching me?" I asked. "Why? Who are you?"

"I'm Eileen. I'm your Watcher," she said quietly with a quick smile that faded.

"Watcher?"

"Yes, whenever we see or hear about someone who shows signs of thinking for themselves, one of us is assigned to watch them and bring them along, so to speak," Eileen said, looking me straight in the eyes.

"Who is 'WE'?" I asked.

"We're the Resistance."

"You mean you're with the Underground? The terrorists and anti-government nonconformists?"

"I'm with people who believe freedom means more than absolute obedience to government gods," she retorted.

"So you're what—a terrorist?"

"I'm an activist."

I snorted. "That's code for troublemaker, and I don't need any more trouble. I'm probably already in enough trouble as it is."

"Trust me, your trouble is only just beginning," she said, her eyes full of regret. "In any case, your friend Lucian tagged you to be watched in case they tried to grab you."

"Lucian? I was in Academy Five with him," I stuttered, starting to stand up. "He never said ... He was detained weeks ago."

"Do you know why he was detained?"

"Do they ever need a reason?" I asked, bitterly. "They pulled him out of class one day. It could have been something he said. Something he did. Maybe he just looked at an Enforcer the wrong way. It doesn't take much."

"No, it doesn't take much," Eileen murmured. "But as one of his friends, you would have hit the suspect list automatically. It was only a matter of time before they started monitoring you for subversive activity."

"How do I know Lucian is really one of you? How do I know you're not just a plant to get me in trouble? Lucian never said a word—"

"Yes, Lucian is one of us. He was waiting until you were ready to know more."

"Know more about what?" I asked. "I don't need to know more."

"Then why did you swipe that package from the dead guy?" Eileen asked.

"How did you know—?"

"Let's just say we have our own ways of watching."

Since I still didn't understand what motivated me to put myself in the crosshairs like that, nor was I prepared to confess anything to someone I'd only just met, I ignored the question.

"Anyway, things are fine," I muttered. "The government keeps us safe, provides for our needs, gives us free education and jobs…" I trailed off, painfully aware of how pitiful I sounded.

"If you believed any of the trash you're spouting, you wouldn't have been hiding in your room with contraband," Eileen countered. "If things are fine, how did you get that scar on the back of your neck? The government didn't protect you from that robofly attack, did it?"

She had me for the moment.

I simply gave her a bland stare.

"You're fighting a losing battle. You can't overthrow the government," I said. "It's too big. It's too powerful. And it's a suicide mission. We humans don't have a chance against the technology. You can't resist an Atlas Four and an army of androids."

"If you believe that, why didn't you turn Lucian in when he told you it was time to resist?"

"How did you know—?" I shrugged my shoulders. "Listen, Lucian and I were friends, but that doesn't mean I agreed with him on everything. We're just little people, and we can't fight the system."

Eileen's eyes sparked. "Well, we'll have to agree to disagree until I can change your mind. For now, you'd better be grateful that there are 'little people' who dare to fight the system, because you're in a heap of trouble. Let's go. It's time to move."

I remained rooted to the spot, torn by indecision. If I followed her, there'd be no turning back. Then again, what choice did I really have? Either way, I was in for trouble. I stood up and eased the kinks out of my legs.

Eileen did the same. "Let's ease out of here before your lobe chip reactivates. We'll head to the sanctuary where you can meet some more of the Resistance."

Eileen slowly opened the door and peeked out.

"All clear," she said, looking over her shoulder. "Follow me."

We moved towards the elevator.

"Put these on," she instructed, handing me a pair of rainbow-lensed glasses and pulling out a pair for herself. "The lenses scatter the light refractions and scramble the biometric scanner readings, so the Controllers won't be able to track you using the facial recognition cameras."

She slid her magic bullet over the pad by the door. With a whoosh, the doors opened. Stepping inside, she remarked, "I've also temporarily disengaged the surveillance cameras in here."

On the way down, my mind raced, crowded with everything Eileen had said to me. The doors opened into the lobby. We walked outside into the teeming streets. It was early evening and the twilight dust was beginning to settle.

CHAPTER 4
THE WORMHOLE

"Watch out for wormholes."—Mitchell Hare

The air was thick.

It was so thick it was hard to breathe.

It was not only filled with the usual polluted brown haze—a result of the chemtrails that crisscrossed the sky throughout the day—but also the foul smells of burned circuitry emitted by the Atlas Fours and various hovering roboflies, gliderbots and the like.

We merged into the crowded sidewalk.

"So are you going to tell me about the parcel that's got you on the run?" Eileen asked, placing an airscape filter over her nasal passages.

"I'm not sure what it is, exactly. A diary of some kind. I haven't really had much time to look at it or figure out what it means."

"Well, maybe Spidus can help," Eileen said, looking straight ahead.

"Spidus?" I asked, attempting to keep my face expressionless.

"Wait and see," she answered.

Above us, roboflies and other spying stalkers filled the skies.

It wasn't only the machines that were watching, however. Everything and virtually everyone watches each other for possible deviations in behavior and reports back. Deviants are always reported to the police.

Lucian's words came whispering back to me: "We are being brainwashed from the time we're born to the time we die to be spies. Spying on one another."

That's when I heard that strange, but familiar, roaring noise.

Half a block ahead, a Rex 84 was carrying something in its massive, cisor-like jaws. When its head turned to the right, I could see that it was a human, a limp human, its bloodied head dangling from one side of the large reptilian jaws. On the other side of the massive jaws, two thin legs wisped back and forth with the rancid breeze.

A terrorist, a criminal, a nonconformist or a rebel, I speculated? They always ended the same way: tortured or dead. That was the punishment for resistance. If you valued your life, you avoided those folks at all costs, and here I was walking in broad daylight with a member of the Resistance.

"Erik, over here," Eileen instructed. "Let's take the Laset to our destination."

"Sure," I replied, shrugging my shoulders.

We walked up a ramp that jetted from the side of the transit vehicle. Following behind Eileen, I settled in beside her on the seat.

"Oh, and be careful. Your biochip will be reconnecting any minute now. So be careful what you think and say until I can activate my magic bullet."

"I'll try," I replied, wondering more about her elaborate toy.

"Here, take this. You're going to need it," she said, as she handed me a nasal filter. "The air only gets worse from here on out." With that, she placed an index finger vertically across her lips. It was time to be quiet.

Peering out the window of the transit, I could see that we were passing street after street filled with bustling stores and jostling crowds. People coming and going, entering and exiting, and I seemed to be on a one-way ticket, but to where?

Eileen motioned that our stop was approaching. The transit came to a stop, and I followed Eileen down the ramp. Turning to our right, we started walking toward a large overhead sign which read, "F-Zone."

The "F" stands for Forbidden.

I stopped in my tracks, painfully aware that I stood on the precipice of a major life change, no matter which way I moved.

"Here, take another dose of this," Eileen said, touching her magic bullet to my forehead. "That should disable your biochip for another eight hours or so."

"Why are we going to F-Zone?" I asked. "That's where the undesirables, anti-socials, outcasts and extremists reside. Aren't I in enough trouble already?"

"Trust me," she said.

"I don't even *know* you," I shot back. "For all I know, you could be a government agent trying to set me up."

"Do I *look* like a government agent?" she asked, a dangerous glint in her eye.

"Well, you don't look like much of a Resistance fighter, either," I said. "In fact, you don't even look old enough to be out of school."

"I'm old enough to know that I don't want to spend what life I have left as a slave to the Controllers," she said. "You're what 17? 18?"

"I'm 19," I replied. "But if I follow where you're headed, I might not make it to 20."

"Living is easy with eyes closed," she murmured. "Can you honestly tell me that you enjoy living in fear, having your thoughts and movements monitored, always having to look over your shoulder, or hide in corners?"

She was starting to awaken thoughts in me—dangerous, liberating, tempting thoughts—that I'd hardly dared to think about lest my biochip give me away.

I shifted uneasily, not quite ready to believe in her or the protection of her magic bullet.

"You ever hear of rabbit holes?" Eileen asked, peering straight ahead.

I raised my eyebrows at her sudden topic change.

"Rabbit holes," she repeated. "Tunnels created by furry little creatures that are now practically extinct. Like the one in Alice in Wonderland?"

"I guess," I replied, still not sure where she was going with this new thread of conversation.

"Well, instead of a tunnel, we're going to be using a wormhole."

"Listen, even your magic bullet can't make me small enough to fit down a hole for maggots," I muttered.

"Wormholes connect the two distinct realities or worlds. This particular wormhole connects the Topsiders with the Subterraneans."

"If you say so," I said.

"First, we've got to get past the F-Zone goon squad," she said.

Two Atlas Fours were stationed at the entrance to F-Zone. On either side of a barbed wire fence, just under the large F-Zone sign, clear directives flashed intermittently, warning that F-Zone is a forbidden area.

Here and there, roboflies buzzed overhead, occasionally emitting laser strikes that hit the ground with a crashing thud.

"Quickly, take my hand," Eileen ordered.

Hand in hand, we walked at a brisk pace down a narrow street that curved away from F-Zone. Several blocks later, out of breath, we arrived at a small, old, red brick building. The sign in the window read "Antique Boutique." Beneath that, "Mitchell Hare, Proprietor."

"Let's step inside," Eileen said, as she opened a squeaking door that creaked even louder as we pushed through it.

The air inside reeked of staleness and mold. An aging bald man with strange bionic eye caverns stood behind a counter, a ghost of a smile playing over his face.

"Hare, the proprietor of this establishment, I assume?" Eileen asked.

"Yes, that would be me," the man replied with a wide toothy grin.

"I've been telling my friend here the old story about the girl who fell down a rabbit hole and landed in a strange, fascinating place," Eileen explained. "You know it, don't you?"

"Know it? Young lady, I live it every day," the bald one said with a laugh. "Old things, that is. Antiquaries are my business. In fact, I have some lovely time pieces that just might interest you."

"Actually, what I'm really looking for is an old teapot for my friend here," Eileen explained, pointing at my frozen, puzzled face.

"Oh yes," the old man replied with a weird shout. "We've got all kinds: tall ones, short ones, stout ones, you name it. They're in the small room down that set of stairs. See what you will find. Just watch out for wormholes."

"Perfect," Eileen said, smiling and signaling for me to follow.

We walked through an aisle lined on both sides with old wheels, wires, chairs and the like. Finally, we came to an old wooden door.

Eileen opened the door to virtual darkness except for a red flashing light at the bottom of a set of stairs. A blinking sign read, "No exit."

"Come," Eileen said. "Spidus awaits."

As she disappeared into the darkness, I followed, closing the door behind me.

CHAPTER 5
SUBTERRANEANS

"Subterranea is the hub of the Resistance movement. Most of the people you saw when we came in are the technos, hackers and the like who monitor the CorpoElite's communication network."—Eileen

We descended a long flight of stairs.

When we reached the bottom, Eileen unlocked an old, rusted steel door by pointing her magic bullet at the "No Exit" screen overhead.

The door slowly opened. Except for a slender beam of light peeking beneath the bottom of another set of doors up ahead, we were in utter darkness.

"Watch your step," Eileen cautioned.

Again, she waved her magic bullet at the small screen device affixed to the right of the second doorway. As it opened, our eyes were blinded by a burst of artificial white light and a clamoring of voices.

Situated in a large common area was an array of desks manned by young techies in ragged clothes, with a few older ones scattered among them.

Flickering screens littered the walls.

"Hey Eileen!" one of the techies shouted, peering over his shoulder. "About time you made it back. We were getting worried."

"We ran into some delays. Where's Ginger?" Eileen asked abruptly.

"He's topside dealing with another riot." The techie pointed to a large screen positioned on the wall just above us. "Probably infiltrators.

Undercover government agents have been mixing with the crowd. Stirring things up. Causing havoc. See, there they are."

Onscreen, a jumble of people were fighting among themselves in total chaos. Bloodied bodies lay strewn about the streets.

"Looks like F-Zone is undergoing its usual carefully choreographed virtual violence," the techie said, now looking at Eileen. "So who's the guy trailing you?"

"This is Erik, a friend of Lucian's," Eileen explained. "Erik, meet Marcel, one of our techies."

"Hey," I said, raising my hand in greeting.

"Welcome to Subterranea," Marcel said, gesturing behind him to the crude, multicolored, hand drawn sign on the wall. Beneath the word "SUBTERRANEA," in faded lettering, it read: "Welcome to Subway Central."

"This area used to be some sort of transit system. F-Zone is located right above..." Marcel stopped midsentence, a puzzled look on his face. "Did you say this guy was a friend of Lucian's?"

"More on that later," Eileen replied. "We need to get with Ginger first. And I need a place for Erik to bunk down."

"Use one of the bunks in your quadrant," Marcel replied. "We're almost at capacity everywhere else."

Eileen steered me over to a small cubicle area populated by a group of cots.

"This will have to do for now," she said as I tested the springs on the narrow bed.

"How long do I have to stay here? And where exactly is here?"

"Subterranea is the hub of the Resistance movement. Most of the people you saw when we came in are the technos, hackers and the like, who monitor the CorpoElite's communication network."

"You mean they spy on the spies?" I asked, with a smirk.

"And their android extensions like the roboflies, Atlases and so on," Eileen said. "With those screens, we can watch through their eyes, see what they say. Of course, when the Controllers do it, it's called surveillance, supposedly to keep the masses safe. When we do it, it's called hacking."

"How do you know they're not looking right back at you?" I asked.

"We don't," she said, shrugging her shoulders. "Nothing is fool-proof. There's a very good chance that they are watching us as well, sort of a reverse mirror effect. So we have to work twice as hard to bounce their signals and baffle their lenses. We've also developed an electromagnetic destabilizer which blocks access to our biochips."

"And you're trying to accomplish what exactly?" I asked, attempting to appear unimpressed by the little I had seen so far in the Underground, which was still far more than anything I had seen attempted topside.

"We're *trying* to shift the balance of power," she retorted, her eyes flashing with heat and outrage. "We're trying to get back to a place where freedom means something more than the freedom to choose between life as a slave to the CorpoElite or certain death as a resistor."

I couldn't help goading her further. "But what's the point? CorpoElite has all the firepower, all the manpower, all the intel. Aren't you fighting a losing battle?"

"If I thought the way you do, I'd already be locked up somewhere, awaiting interrogation, torture or re-education," Eileen said with a disgusted glare. "The point is that even overpowered, outmanned and outgunned, we'd still risk our lives to fight a losing battle if it means we might be able to break some of the chains that bind us to our overlords, regain even an iota of control over our own lives and awaken some of the sleeping populace. Who knows, we might even manage to save some of our fellow humans, even if they are clueless like you."

"About that..." I stuttered, tongue-tied and suddenly ashamed. "I...ah...I didn't mean to sound ungrateful. I mean, I know you saved my neck back there. It's just..."

Shaking her head, Eileen cuffed me on the shoulder. "A thank you will suffice."

"Yo," Marcel interrupted, peeking around the corner of our cubicle. "The riot has subsided, so Ginger should be returning soon."

"Great," Eileen said. "Let him know I need to see him ASAP, will you?"

"Can do," Marcel replied. Shifting his eyes in my direction, he asked, "What's your story? You on the lam?"

"Sorry, bro, but this one's hot," Eileen interrupted. "I'm under orders to keep him under wraps until he can report directly to Spidus."

"A special delivery for Spidus, huh?" Marcel scrutinized me more closely. "You can't get much hotter than that. I'll make sure Ginger gets the message."

Waiting until Marcel had turned and walked away, Eileen sat next to me on the cot. She smelled sweet and warm. Her skin was like golden amber. I suddenly felt warm all over.

"Can I see the parcel?" Eileen asked.

"Hmmm? What parcel?" I murmured, realizing that her eyes, dark from a distance, were like molten pools of chocolate up close.

"The package that started all this trouble," she said, looking at me as if I'd lost my mind.

"Oh right, *that* package. Sure, here it is." I pulled it out from inside my outerwear and handed it over.

CHAPTER 6
GINGER

"Pull a gun on me again woman and I'll shove it up your behind."—Ginger

Eileen slid her index finger under the flap on the parcel, pulled out the collection of pages and unfolded them.

Her eyes scanned the pages slowly, her lips moving slightly as she read, her entire being focused on what was before her. I could just as well have burst into flames beside her and she might not have noticed, she was so absorbed in the hastily scrawled diary.

"This guy was interrogated by a Werewolf Unit," she murmured, almost to herself.

"What's a Werewolf Unit?" I asked.

"What?" she asked, looking up reluctantly.

"You said the guy was interrogated by a Werewolf Unit. What is it?"

"They're militarily trained police teams that focus on troublemakers. One of their specialties is home raids. Crashing through doors in the middle of the night. They're known for terrorizing people. They have special operations officers who act as interrogators. That's probably who worked this guy over," she said.

"So you think he's for real, then?" I asked.

"What I've read so far is unlike anything I've ever read before, but it doesn't read like a plant to me," she said. "Spidus would know more, though."

Without warning, Eileen slapped the manuscript into my hands and shifted so that she stood squarely in front of me.

"Marcel says you're looking for me," a gruff voice said.

"Ginger!" Eileen exclaimed, moving to embrace a thin man clothed in little more than rags. "You look really stressed."

"Yeah, it was pretty rough up there. The Intels and Werewolves stirred up a mess. They infiltrated some of the resistance units and got us fighting one another again," Ginger said, taking a deep breath. "Divide and conquer. It seems to work every time."

Looking at him, I was struck by his haggard appearance. His face sported a scruffy beard and was blotched with dirt and grime. His lips looked torn and his teeth appeared to be barbed wire.

"They're infiltrating everything, including this place. I mean, some of the folks down here with us have to be Intels," Ginger griped.

"So they know we're here?" I asked. "Can they raid this place?"

Ginger peered around Eileen, who still stood squarely between us, and glared at me before turning his attention back to Eileen. "Who is this guy?" he huffed. "And why is he talking to me?"

"This is Erik. He was a friend of Lucian's," she explained, angling her body so she once again stood squarely between me and Ginger. "I brought him here."

"And you did this why?" Ginger asked pointedly. "Do we need yet another mole in this place? Don't we have enough already?"

"He's not a mole. I told you, he's the friend of Lucian's I was assigned to shadow," Eileen said. "He swiped a parcel off the street after it was dropped by a dying man. It set off his P2P alarm for a violation and it looks like they set the droids on him, so I brought him here until we figure out what's going on."

"So he's not too smart AND he's a mole," Ginger growled.

"Shut it, Ginger," Eileen ordered. Turning to me, she grimaced. "Ignore him, Erik. He was the leader of a Werewolf Unit before he defected, so he's got some trust issues."

"You were a Werewolf?" I asked.

"What's it to you?" Ginger retorted, looking me over once again. "What do you know about the Werewolves?"

"Not much, other than what I read in these pages," I said, returning his look of disdain.

"Let me see that," Ginger said, grabbing the pages before Eileen could protest.

He read quickly, eyes skimming over the words. Halfway through the second page, he stopped, shoved the pages at Eileen, grabbed me by the collar and slammed me down on the bed. "This guy's an Intel. You don't get hold of information like this unless you're one of them," Ginger growled, straddling me with his first raised like a hammer.

The blow cracked across my face. The pain was unbelievable. I saw stars. Then Eileen stepped in.

"Enough, Ginger!" she ordered as she shoved Ginger off the side of the bed. He fell with a thud only to spring up again, ready to pummel me more.

"Stop it, I said!" This time, Eileen was pointing a small weapon at Ginger. "Back off. You're wrong. He's no mole."

"You know we've been infiltrated. You know they know we're watching them. You know they're watching us," Ginger spat out. "What better cover than to send a rat into our midst claiming to need our protection," he said, giving me a hostile look.

"Spidus gave me this assignment, so it's his call," Eileen growled, still pointing her weapon at my assailant. "Let's see what Spidus thinks before you go off half-cocked."

"Sure. Spidus will know," Ginger said, wiping some spittle from his mouth. "But stay alert, 'cos your new friend might just turn foe when you least expect it."

"My middle name is alert," Eileen retorted with a sassy grin.

"Yeah, yeah, I've heard that one before," Ginger said, shaking his head at her, before breaking into a rueful grin. "Pull a gun on me again woman, and I'll shove it up your behind."

Eileen snorted. "You're all talk, G-man."

"That's Mr. G-man to you, kid," he said, "As for you, you piece of crap," he said, with a squinty-eyed stare directed at me, "I've got my eye on you."

CHAPTER 7
SPIDUS

"Yes, we are the walking dead until we awake to the truth. Truth is a weapon, a weapon that the Controllers fear. That's why they do all they can to distract you and keep you asleep."—Spidus

My life among the Resistance was not getting off to a promising start.

"I'll take this to Spidus," Ginger growled as he snatched up the contraband, turned and walked away.

"And I should trust this guy why?" I asked, watching Ginger's retreating back until he disappeared around a corner.

"Ginger is one of Spidus' most trusted advisors and chief bodyguard."

"If HE is one of Spidus' most trusted advisors, it doesn't say much about Spidus," I replied, rubbing my aching jaw, stewing over the blow Ginger had landed.

Eileen punched me in the shoulder.

"Ow!" I cried, more surprised than hurt.

"You want to trash talk Ginger, that's fine. He usually deserves it," she spat out. "But Spidus is off limits."

"All I said was—"

"All you said was enough to show that you're basically a clueless, brainless, unteachable moron lacking even the most rudimentary common sense to know that if it weren't for Spidus taking an interest in you— Spidus assigning me to shadow you—Spidus risking the operation's cover in order to save your neck, you'd be dead or worse by now," she fired back at me.

"There's not much worse you can get than dead," I pointed out.

"Trust me," she said, drilling a finger into my chest, "there are far worse things than being dead, especially if the Controllers get hold of you."

She had me there.

Of course, I'd heard rumors of what the Controllers did to people accused of being anti-government or domestic terrorists.

The rumors were bad stuff. Bad enough to convince most citizens to walk the straight and narrow and never do anything, say anything or think anything that might put them on the government's radar.

"You're right," I admitted, holding up my hands in surrender and conceding the point. "I'm an idiot. But I assure you that I'm a grateful idiot."

Eileen laughed and curled up into a corner of the cot, feet tucked under her.

"So who is Spidus exactly?" I asked.

"Spidus? He's the heart and soul of the Resistance. Without him to guide and advise us, I don't know where we'd be," Eileen replied.

"So he's like a priest or something?" I asked.

Eileen laughed again. "Spidus probably falls more into the 'or something' category. He's the last of the early resistors and the only living person among us who remembers a time when the CorpoElite wasn't in absolute total control."

"So he's ancient?"

"No one knows exactly how old he is, but he's what you'd consider a general, I suppose," Eileen explained. "He's the reason we're all here."

"And he's the reason I'm here?"

"Well, I suppose Lucian is the one who really started the ball rolling, but yes, Spidus gave the orders for me to shadow you," Eileen said.

"You talk as if you know Lucian personally."

"Once, I knew Lucian very well." A troubled look passed over her face and then was gone. "He's my brother."

"Lucian is your brother? He never mentioned a sister..."

Eileen grinned, and in her grin, I saw Lucian.

"Well, Lucian was always a great one for keeping secrets," she said with a shrug. "He could talk your head off and still say nothing at all."

Just then Ginger walked up.

"Spidus will see the boy now," Ginger said, staring down his nose at me. "But be warned: don't move a muscle unless you're given the go-ahead first. Speak clearly and look Spidus in the eye when you talk to him. And you tell him exactly what he wants to know. His body might be broken, but his mind is like a laser beam."

"Looks like it's showtime," Eileen said, stretching the kinks out of shoulders.

"Are you coming, too?" I asked her, doing my best to avoid Ginger's glare.

"Don't worry, your girlfriend can come and hold your hand," Ginger smirked. "But I'm the one walking you through that door to meet the man. Depending on if you're playing this straight or not, it's either the door to paradise or the door to hell, kid. So say a little prayer. You may need it."

Eileen and I trailed Ginger down a short hallway, then down a small flight of stairs. Stopping before a faded, green door, Ginger knocked, took a deep breath, then turned the knob slowly.

As the door opened, the burning smell of chemicals washed over me. My eyes began to water.

Stepping inside, I saw a hospital bed situated directly across a large empty room. Tubes fed into a supine human body. Monitors flashed and made weird buzzing noises.

Situated on the walls were three large telescreens. One beamed cityscape images, interior rooms and hallways. Stats flickered in the corner of the screen. Constantly changing images ranging from Atlas Fours patrolling the streets to haze-filled skies cluttered another. Circling gliderbots were plastered on the third.

Placing his arm on my shoulder, Ginger frog-marched me to the bed-side. "Spidus, this is Erik Blair, the kid we just rescued. The one with the manuscript."

"Ah, the contraband," replied Spidus.

"Ancient" didn't come close to describing him. This man was older than old. What hair he still had on his head was long, white, and sparse. An equally scant gray beard covered his face in patches. Yet it was his skin, the parts not covered by the blue hospital gown, that forced my eyes to focus more clearly.

Dark red splotches emanated from a spiderweb of needles and tubes that seemed to almost encase him in a cocoon.

"So you're Erik Blair?" he murmured, his amber eyes piercing me.

"Yes, sir," I said, unsure whether to salute or stand at attention.

"You're fortunate to be alive, Mr. Blair," Spidus intoned. "The manuscript you found would have marked you for death or worse had you been captured."

"Yeah, I get that," I said. "I owe you big time."

"Well, I'll keep that in mind," Spidus said with the hint of a smile. "You may get a chance to re-pay that debt in kind one of these days."

"Sure, yeah, just say the word," I replied with a little more enthusiasm than I was feeling.

Spidus' smile was bigger this time. "Patience, young grasshopper," he cautioned.

I glanced over at Eileen, unsure how to respond to being likened to a long-legged insect.

"Ah, forgive me," Spidus said, intercepting my look. "I meant no offense. The phrase is a relic of my childhood. It's what the old mage would say to the young apprentice in *Kung Fu*."

I still didn't get it.

"Did you know that dreams about grasshoppers portend freedom, independence, and spiritual enlightenment?" Spidus asked. "All things in short supply right now. Which brings me to your manuscript and how it happened to fall into your hands."

"Yeah, it was pretty random," I said. "Guess it was my unlucky day."

"Unlucky? Random?" Spidus squinted over at me. "There was nothing random or unlucky about it, Erik. We've analyzed a bit of the manuscript. It's an amazing document, a critical key to the future by a prophet of the past."

"You mean it's more than just a rambling diary by some torture victim?" I asked, only to have Eileen jab me in the ribs and glare in my direction.

"Quite a bit more, I would say. How much of it did you read?" Spidus asked.

I grimaced. "Not much. Just a page or two before the P2P alarm went off."

"Well, I would strongly advise you to read more of it. There's a reason it was delivered to you, and it would behoove us to know why you were singled out."

I started stuttering. I couldn't help it. "Spidus, sir, I … ah … think you were misinformed. The papers weren't delivered to me. I just happened to be at the wrong place at the wrong time when this guy keeled over on the sidewalk."

Spidus started to laugh. Or maybe he was choking. I couldn't really tell.

Ginger reached out to prop him up so he could catch his breath, only to be waved away. "I'm fine, Ginger. Stop fussing for a minute. So," Spidus said, turning to me once again, "you think you were in the wrong place at the wrong time?"

"Sure," I shrugged. "It was just dumb luck."

"I'll second the dumb part," Ginger muttered under his breath, only to have Eileen give him a warning jab in the ribs. At least I wasn't the only one on the receiving end of her disapproval.

"What if I told you that, in fact, you *were* singled out?" Spidus asked. "What if I told you that you were in exactly the right place at the right time, and that you were meant to get these papers, meant to trigger your P2P, meant to become an outlaw, meant to be welcomed into the fold of the Resistance?"

"No offense, sir," I said, "but I'm pretty sure there's nothing special about me to warrant that much of a conspiracy."

"Well, I suppose we can debate the vagaries of fate another time," Spidus said. "For now, I can tell you that the author of your manuscript— or diary—or contraband—or whatever term you want to use for it was a man by the name of George Orwell, who lived during the mid-20th century."

"And you know this how?" I asked.

"Although there is no name identifier on the manuscript, the hand-writing and style are very much Orwell's. There's even a DNA match, although our sources indicate the DNA was from that guy you saw drop dead, which doesn't compute, but I have a theory about that."

"Am I supposed to know this guy?" I asked.

"George Orwell used to be quite well known when there was still some concept of freedom among the masses. But when the Controllers assumed control, that knowledge and the writings of anyone who could inspire revolt were carefully eliminated," Spidus explained with a wince, as if in pain.

"Eliminated?" I asked.

"Eliminated. Deleted. Cleansed. Erased from the databanks and history books. There are others, names you've heard of, who have been reduced to statues in cities and parks, their controversial words or writings deleted. Deceptions in stone is what I call them," Spidus explained. "The only traces of them left behind are the so-called 'nice' things they said or did. Words that don't challenge authority, acts that don't defy, history that serves only to feed the myth of obedience to government."

Spidus paused to gasp for breath. "Some writers used to see the future and try to awaken those on the battlefield of the dead with the truth."

"The battlefield of the dead?" I asked, glancing quickly at Eileen to see her reaction.

"Yes, we are the walking dead until we awaken to the truth. Truth is a weapon, a weapon that the Controllers fear. That's why they do all they can to distract you and keep you asleep. The battlefield is always about the truth, but most never realize it until it's too late," Spidus said, his voice weakening.

Taking another deep breath, Spidus continued, "When all knowledge was digitized, the Controllers began to edit history and literature as they saw fit, redacting anything that could be interpreted as radical or subversive and leaving only that which is safe."

"But there were those like Orwell who sensed what was coming and tried to send a warning to those of us in the future," Spidus said, now raised up on his elbows and looking at me with a penetrating stare. "I believe—although this is only my theory—that what you grabbed up off the street was Orwell's final warning to the future, personally delivered to you by Orwell himself."

"The guy really didn't look old enough to be—" I did some quick calculations in my head, "—200 years old."

"I would expect not," Spidus replied. "We know that Orwell ended his life in a coma, and endured a horrible, painful death. But we cannot rule out the possibility that Orwell may have mastered other means of communicating with the future. Time travel, perhaps."

"Time travel?" I repeated.

"Yes, time travel. Although those in a coma are in a suspended state of animation, their minds are still active and alert," Spidus said. "And the mind, as we now know, radiates outside the body and can live on even after death."

Talk about mind-blowing. I had no idea what Spidus was getting at. Even Eileen seemed taken aback.

"How Orwell managed it is fascinating to contemplate, but immaterial," Spidus said, scanning my face carefully. "What we must figure out is why he chose you, of all people, and why he chose to appear to you in this moment in time. There may be a genetic connection, which would solve the first part of the puzzle."

"Are you saying I'm related to this guy?" I asked, wide-eyed.

"Perhaps," came Spidus' reply. "Or perhaps you are a genetic messenger, of sorts. It may be that you have some form of memory stored in your DNA, just waiting for the right key to open the door. Perhaps this diary is the key."

"But why now, Spidus?" Eileen asked.

"Well, it is 2084, a century after Orwell's novel *1984* was set," Spidus ruminated, rubbing his chin. "Orwell predicted the future would resemble a boot stamping on a human face forever. It's an apt metaphor for our world today, under the dictates of the Controllers. Perhaps Orwell figured we could use a little help."

"So to sum up: you think a guy who died over a hundred years ago planted a DNA memory in me and then somehow traveled through time in order to appear on a public sidewalk in the middle of a crowded city surrounded by roboflies and gliderbots and a million government eyes in order to deliver a diary to me that will somehow unlock a vault in my mind and provide you with information that will help you to take down the Controllers?" I asked, my voice strained.

Ginger scowled.

Spidus beamed. "That just about sums it up."

Before I could respond, Eileen grabbed my arm and squeezed. Hard.

"This is a lot for Erik to take in right now," Eileen interrupted apologetically. "Can we give him some time to process all of this before we dump anything more on him?"

"Yes, that might be wise," Spidus said, giving me an understanding look. Then smiling a bit, Spidus said, "Ginger, give Erik a copy of the document. We can talk again once you've read it."

Ginger handed the manuscript over, a look of distaste on his face and a clear insult ready to trip off his lips, only to knock me sideways with a growl and brace himself in front of Spidus as someone opened the door.

"Tumor's at it again," a voice shouted. "He just smashed someone in the face. Blood's flying!"

"It's that nut job again who beat his wife's head in with a can of soup," Ginger said, adopting a more relaxed stance and stepping back from Spidus' bedside. "I've about had it with him, freedom fighter or not."

Grabbing my arm, Ginger led me and Eileen through the doorway and down the stairs where two men were being held apart forcefully, one bleeding profusely from the mouth.

CHAPTER 8
THE ZOMBIE ROOM

"If you weren't programmed, you would awaken to the fact that life is a waking nightmare. You'd get fed up very quickly with pollution, violence and a general populace who live their lives as if they were sleepwalkers or well-fed cows on their way to the slaughterhouse."—Spidus

Ginger took off at a full gallop.

Shoving the bleeding guy to safety, he stood squarely in front of the brawling man. "Tumor, back off!"

"But he accused me of murdering my wife!" Tumor screamed. The muscled warrior of a man began weeping uncontrollably.

"Here. Go with Murry. He'll get you something to settle you down," Ginger said.

A young techie stepped forward to lead Tumor away.

"But he laughed and said I was crazy!" Tumor screamed, again facing his opponent. "I'm tired of this stuff, man!"

Ginger shifted once again, placing himself directly between Tumor and his opponent. "This is your final warning: get out of here, or I'll take you down myself, Tumor."

"Tumor, listen to him. Please," Eileen entreated, laying a gentle hand on his arm.

The mountain of a man shuddered with emotion, hung his head in defeat and nodded.

"All right," Tumor said, taking a deep breath and departing with Murry.

"So this guy murdered his wife with a can of soup and he's allowed to move freely down here because—?" I asked.

"Because everyone needs a second chance," Eileen said, still staring at Tumor's retreating back. "Besides, *HE* didn't murder his wife. He was being mind-controlled by the Controllers at the time. Making him kill his wife was how the Controllers punished him for resisting their demands."

"Resisting what demands?" I asked.

"Why do you care?" Ginger asked. After a silent glare from Eileen, he shrugged and explained: "Tumor is a tech wiz. He can decipher virtually any encrypted messages. He refused to help the Controllers crack the code the Resistance uses for its communications. So now we give him sanctuary and when he's lucid, he helps us stay off the Controllers' radar."

"Yo, Ginger," a bearded, gray-haired man tugged at Ginger's elbow. "Spidus wants you back in his quarters. Something's going down. And he wants you to bring those two," he said, with a nod in our direction.

"What the hell is it now? We were just there," Ginger groused as he did an about-face and began marching toward Spidus' control center/convalescence room complex. "Step on it, you two. Do I look like I have all day to dawdle?"

The moment we entered Spidus' quarters, the old man beckoned us closer, pointing up at the screens. "Ginger, it is as we feared."

On the screens, plastered to the walls, a man was squirming and doing his best to resist as he was led away by two Atlas Fours on either side of him. They were headed toward a large set of double doors. Overhead, a sign in dark red letters read: "Violence Reduction Center."

Eileen uttered a small cry and stepped closer to the screens. Ginger followed her with his eyes, but made no move to approach her.

"Recognize him, Erik?" Spidus asked.

All I could see was the guy's back as he was being dragged—occasionally carried—towards the ominous looking metal doors. But there was something familiar about him. The long hair hanging down over his shoulder. And that walk.

I glanced over at Eileen, who was shaking and pale.

The knowledge, when it hit me, was more painful than the sucker punch Ginger had delivered earlier.

"That's Lucian, isn't it?" I asked.

Spidus glanced over at Eileen's silent form. "Yes, that is Lucian."

"Where are they taking him? What's going on?"

Spidus grimaced. "If our suppositions are correct, Lucian is being taken to what we in the movement refer to as a Zombie Room."

"A what?" I exclaimed.

"A Zombie Room, or a ZRoom, is where they—agents of the Controllers—carry out what they refer to as positive reprogramming," Spidus explained.

"Are they going to brainwash him or something?" I asked, unable to look away from Lucian, who continued to struggle as he was dragged through the double doors.

"If only it were as simple as that," Spidus replied. "While I understand there are those among the masses who pay to have their memories erased, preferring to sleepwalk through life, they will not stop at merely removing Lucian's memories. They are going to attempt to rewire him altogether."

"They're going to do a prefrontal lobotomy on Lucian," Eileen said, only turning towards us once Lucian had disappeared behind the doors. "They'll drive him mad with pain and then they'll turn him into a monster. We won't ever see our Lucian again."

"But there's got to be something we can do to help him?" I protested.

Eileen glanced over at me, dry-eyed. "He's beyond our reach. Nothing can help him now."

"We have some captured footage of a lobotomy conducted not too long ago," Spidus said. "If you have the stomach for it, it would be wise for you to understand what exactly we're up against."

I gave a half-hearted shrug.

"Ginger, set it up," Spidus ordered.

"Yeah. Let me grab the controls," a harried Ginger replied, reaching for a remote. "Maybe Eileen should skip this. She's seen it already anyhow."

"No," Eileen said. "I won't turn away from it. Not now. Not when he's about to go under the knife."

Ginger looked as if he wanted to argue, but only nodded and began fiddling with different controls on one of the computers.

"There is no sound," Spidus said as the screen flickered, then filled with grainy pixels. Overhead cameras zoomed in on a man lying face up on a giant operating table. He was jerking his eyes from side to side. People in white coats lined the table, staring down at him.

"Ravenscrag will be stepping in at any moment. He's the head surgeon or, if you like, butcher," Spidus said, staring at the screen. "You'll see what I mean."

Just then, a man dressed in a black operating outfit stepped forward from the shadows with two large needlelike instruments, one in each hand.

"That's Ravenscrag," Spidus said, looking at me.

The patient on the table began to jerk back and forth shaking his head as if pleading with the surgeon not to proceed.

His mouth was open wide. He was screaming.

"Ravenscrag doesn't like anesthetics," Spidus said, staring at the screen. "They say he likes to see his victims squirm. That's the rumor, anyway."

Ravenscrag's face was covered in a black mask except for his eyes. The camera momentarily froze on his face. His eyes were pitch black. There was no white around his dark pearls.

Ravenscrag motioned with his hands for the aides to back away from the table.

The man on the table—strapped down so that movement was nearly impossible—began to squirm.

"Get ready," Spidus announced.

"Wait a minute," Ginger interrupted. "Do you really need to see this, Eileen?"

"Even if I look away from this screen, now, I'll never be able to stop seeing it in my mind, knowing that these are Lucian's last moments of humanity," Eileen replied. "If Lucian is being made to suffer like this, how can I not suffer too?"

The surgeon on the screen signaled with the flick of his eyes to his aides. Two stepped forward, one on each side of the patient's head. Holding a large cup-shaped device, they slid it under his struggling chin. Next a strap was placed over his forehead.

"Here comes the stab!" Spidus said with a slight grimace on his face.

Ravenscrag slowly inserted one of the needles into the side of the patient's right eye. The patient's mouth was like a large screaming canyon now. Pain wracked his face.

"That's Ravenscrag's surgical technique. He plunges the needle into the edge of the eye to break through the back of the socket," Spidus noted. "As you noticed, he stabbed the eyeball suddenly. Now he moves the needle from side to side cutting the prefrontal lobe of the brain. The pain is excruciating."

Eileen, stoic for most of the procedure, finally broke down with a strangled sob.

"Enough!" I ordered.

"Freeze the show for a moment, Ginger," Spidus commanded as the images came to a halt.

Giving Eileen a moment to compose herself, he resumed his lecturing tone. "As I said, many of the masses voluntarily opt to have their memories erased, which is a far different cry from the brutality of a lobotomy, which does not just erase the past but transforms the person. But more on that later. The pampered masses pay to get the drugs, nice music playing in the background and pretty paintings on the walls during the operation," Spidus said. "You can convince most people of anything once you program them from cradle to grave with virtual connectedness. And, of course, they all have biovoid chips in their prefrontal lobes."

"I thought the biovoid chips were for surveillance," I said.

"The chips aren't just for tracking you, kid," Spidus said, staring up at me from his bed. "They're also brain inhibitors and brain stimulators. That way, the Controllers can read your thoughts, which means they can read your mind. For instance, what do you dream about, Erik? Good dreams? Bad dreams? Do you wake feeling hopeful?"

"Actually, I do wake feeling pretty upbeat," I said. "My dreams are all pretty much the same: meadows, flowers, sunshine, smiling people."

"But none of that exists now. The environment has been destroyed," Spidus said, staring at me. "The pretty dream pictures are what you've been fed through your chips. Nightmares are the truth. They wake you up. But the Controllers don't want you to wake up. If you weren't programmed, you would awaken to the fact that life is a waking nightmare. You'd get fed up very quickly with pollution, violence and a general populace who live their lives as if they were sleepwalkers or well-fed cows on their way to the slaughterhouse."

I stared at Spidus, horrified.

"Okay, Ginger. Let's see the final scene," Spidus said, pointing to the screen.

"Sure thing, boss," Ginger replied with a quick glance at Eileen, who stood quietly near Spidus' bed, his hand resting on hers.

The show resumed as Ravenscrag jiggled the large probe back and forth. The patient continued to scream. Then, suddenly, the patient stopped moving. His mouth closed, his clenched eyes opened, and he smiled slightly.

The screens fell to darkness

"Well, the patient's a new man, Erik," Spidus said. "He won't be causing any trouble now. This black sheep will now fall in line and march in lockstep with the wishes of the Controllers."

I couldn't move, couldn't get a grip on what I had seen, what awaited Lucian.

"That's enough mind bombs for now," Spidus declared. "Eileen, take our young comrade back to your rest area. His awakening is just beginning. Ginger, let the others know that Lucian the Resistor is no more. Tonight, we mourn him and honor his courage. Tomorrow, we seek justice for him and ensure that his sacrifice was not in vain."

CHAPTER 9
RUMPELSTILTSKIN

"The Controllers know very well that people will line up for the concentration camps as long as they provide screen devices, shopping malls and chain restaurants."—Rumpelstiltskin

I tried my best to sleep, but I couldn't turn off my mind or stop imagining the torture Lucian had to be undergoing.

Finally, after staring at the ceiling for longer than I cared to count, I sat up and turned to find Eileen also wide awake. She was lying on her small, ragged bed, reading the manuscript.

"How far have you gotten?" I asked.

"Just skimming," she replied. "I can't seem to focus."

"I couldn't sleep," I said, taking a deep breath. "I just want to punch something or somebody. Anything is better than just sitting here while Lucian suffers."

"How do you think I feel?" she asked, the shine of unshed tears making her eyes glimmer. "He's my brother. He's always protected me. And when he needs me most, I can't do a thing to protect him."

"Man, I *am* an idiot. I'm not helping things much, am I?"

"You're going to be a bigger help than you know," she replied, taking my hand. "Come on."

"Where are we going?"

"I want you to meet someone."

Still holding my hand, Eileen walked me past the bunking area and through the control room. It was lit up from the multi-screens dotting the walls of the complex.

"Yo Eileen, you taking a romantic stroll with your new boyfriend?" called one of the techies, feet propped up on the desk while staring at a screen overhead. "Ginger might get jealous."

"Stick it, Monkey Boy," Eileen retorted. "You've got bigger things to worry about than my love life. Like what Ginger's going to do when he sees you taking a siesta when you should be on patrol."

That wiped the grin off his face fast. With a quick look to make sure Ginger was nowhere around, Monkey Boy sat up at attention and focused his eyes on the flickering screens.

Eileen continued to hold my hand.

Opening a set of double doors, she led me down a narrow hallway full of dark empty offices. Opening another set of double doors, she pointed towards a strange, bridge-like structure that stood at the end of a large room.

"Destination ahead," she said.

In the distance, two figures huddled beneath a multicolored structure. Lights flickered underneath it as we approached.

"Erik, let me introduce you to Jim Keith and his wife Gretel," Eileen said. The man slowly turned his head towards me. "They live here under the rainbow bridge."

"Not another brain-racked fugitive, Eileen. Give me a break, will ya?" Keith begged, rolling his eyes.

"Jim is one of our resident mind analysts, but you can call him Rump," Eileen said. "Jim, this is Erik Blair."

"Rump?" I repeated.

"Short for Rumpelstiltskin," Rump said, with a hard glint in his eye. "You got a problem with that?"

"Stand down, Rump," Eileen interjected, stepping between us. "It's been a rough day. They've taken Lucian to the Zombie Room."

Rump's craggy face appeared to crumple even further. "I was afraid of that," he said, his head dipping down low to his chest. "He was a good man, and a great friend, and a valuable member of the Resistance."

"Lucian was Erik's friend, as well," Eileen added.

Rump's head came up and he looked straight into my eyes. "I'm sorry for your loss."

"We didn't *lose* Lucian! He's not dead! He's being butchered!"

"Erik, calm down," Eileen ordered.

"How can I calm down? How can I listen patiently and talk rationally about anything anymore?"

"You'll do it because you have to," a hoarse, quiet voice said. "Your choices are limited: you can either fight for your right to life or resign yourself to a painful existence as a slave of the Controllers."

It was a voice that sounded as if it rarely got used anymore and it came from the vicinity of Rump's wife, Gretel. Her lips barely seemed to be moving, her face remained downcast, her head hanging down, but she seemed compelled to speak.

"You sit down, boy, and you listen to what Rump has to say," Gretel said. "When nothing makes sense, you have to listen even harder. You can't save Lucian now—he is as good as dead—but you can make sure he didn't lose his freedom for nothing."

A soft hand touched my arm. Eileen pulled me down next to her, her eyes bright with unshed tears and an unspoken grief that put my own to shame.

"You know why they call me Rumpelstiltskin?" Rump asked. "It's because I live under a rainbow bridge, look like a goblin, and can disrupt the Controller's emissions. See that dark gray stuff lining the ceiling of the bridge?"

Scanning the undercoated bridge, I nodded.

"That's lead. It blocks the electromagnetic rays flying every which way and aimed at us by the Controllers. The rays are picked up by the chip implants in our heads, which is how they implant ideas and images in our minds," he remarked, stopping to stare me straight in the eyes. "They also alter our DNA structure with the rays. This way, they can change our essence and make us into what they want. Compliant, crazy, idiotic or whatever suits them."

"They also call him Rumpelstiltskin because he's known for stealing babies and hiding them here under the bridge," Gretel interjected.

"You get them young enough, they might actually have a chance to free their minds," he said with a shrug. "Once the Controllers get their hands on them—once they get those chips implanted—they're doomed."

"What do you do with the babies?" I asked.

Rump glanced at Eileen, who hesitated a moment, shook her head and looked away. "That's on a need-to-know basis, I'm afraid."

"Stop rambling, old man," Gretel ordered.

Rump shrugged again. "Anyway, for whatever reason, I was implanted with an inclusive multi-chip. Most likely a mistake. It differs from your prefrontal lobe chips in that I pick up everything being beamed through the air—not just what is directed at us. I also get access to everything the Controllers put out for their own uses."

"And they never caught on?"

"I learned survival early on. Still, all that clutter and clatter in your brain will drive you nuts. I had to learn how to filter through all of the different signals coming my way. I guess you could call me a human tuning fork."

"So how did you get hooked up with the Resistance?"

Gretel stood up abruptly and shuffled to the opposite end of the bridge. Rump watched her walk away, tears forming in his eyes.

"She's a tough woman," he explained, "but she's never gotten over losing her babies."

"You had kids?"

"We had twins. Once they were old enough, the Controllers were going to take them—as they take all kids—for reprogramming and early indoctrination. We wanted to protect them, but we didn't know what to do, where to go. So we tried to do our own counter-programming. We waited too late. They had already been conditioned to obey without question. They turned us in."

"Your own kids turned you in?"

"They learned their lessons well. And then to punish us for attempting to undermine the system, the Controllers forced us to watch our kids being turned into zombies."

I didn't know what to say. I had heard of things like that happening—I mean, we were all taught to See Something, Say Something in school—but I'd never thought about what happened to the victims of the government's snitch programs after they'd been reported.

Rump glanced over to where Gretel paced and fell into a troubled silence.

"Rump and Gretel were some of the earliest members of the Resistance," Eileen said. "They're also part of the reason we now have a blocker for deprogramming and disabling the bio-chips."

"No blocker for my chip, though," Rump reminded Eileen. "I'm too useful as a receptor. That's why some of the good folks down here built me this small bridge. It blocks most of the signals but not all of them. That means I can now sleep some nights without my mind being bombarded with the Controllers' brain-washing techniques."

"So why don't you just disable everyone's chips at once?" I asked. "Wouldn't that defeat the Controllers?"

"If only it were that simple, kid. You see, the chips are just communication devices. They can't control you unless you've been trained to ignore your own impulses and obey the Controllers without question. By the time most people get to a certain age, their brains have become hard-wired for compliance."

"What Rump means is that most people don't want to be de-programmed," Eileen interjected. "They like their prison walls. The ones who don't—who try to break free—don't always succeed."

"I've seen many freedom fighters caught in the jaws of the governmental machine," Rump added, his eyes staring blankly ahead into the void. "One was my youngest brother. Ed was a good kid. When he freed his mind, he saw that he had been lied to all of his life. Finally, he started listening to me. That's when he joined the Resistance."

"Your brother was part of the movement?" I asked.

"Yes. Ed had only been with us a few weeks before he was captured by a Werewolf Unit. He was 16."

"So what happened to him?" I asked, incredulous.

"They did to him what they're doing to Lucian. They tried to turn him into a zombie. For some reason, it didn't take."

"That's a good thing, right?"

"When that didn't work, they did a vivisection on him while he was still conscious. They gutted him like he was an animal," Rump said, his voice breaking and tears welling up in his eyes. "The only way I kept my head together was to pledge to bring those evil bastards down someday."

Rump was now glaring at me, his voice breaking. "The lesson for you is this: if I could endure that, then you sure as hell can do the same. You've got something to fight for. Remember that."

I nodded, unable to speak.

"C'mon, let's go for a walk. I can step out from beneath my protective shield if I wear this," Rump said, holding a bright, metallic helmet. "This will block most of the electrohits from the Controllers."

He placed the helmet on his head, tightly secured with a chinstrap.

"You see, kid, what's happening inside your head is not all bad. It's forcing you to reconsider some things," Rump said, his arm around my shoulders.

"Erik, I'll see you back at the control room," Eileen said. "I'm going to stay with Gretel for a while."

Rump and I began to walk and talk.

"Most of us are zombies, walking robotically along staring at our screen devices as if it all means something. The point is: it doesn't. Unless you wake up and realize where and who you really are. But the Controllers want to keep you asleep. They want you dependent and needy and cowering. Most of all, they want you compliant. They start by draining the empathy from you. When they control your passions, they can control you. Control is what it's all about. And it starts with your mind."

"Like the programming in school," I interjected.

"Not only that. With all the screen technology that surrounds us, the Controllers have access to our heads—always subliminally feeding something into our conscious and unconscious minds," he emphasized. "And with the implanted brain chips, we have no idea of what's being fed into our heads. I mean, with this multichip in my head, I pick up what's being broadcast to the masses. One day it's 'hate those not like you' or 'it's time to grab a weapon and riot' or 'turn your neighbor in for any violation, no matter how small.' It's hate that allows them to manipulate us to rise up in violence. They love it. When we're violent, they point their fingers and say, 'Look, we've got to be armed to the teeth to keep order.' Violence is their energizer and one way they control the masses is through our violence and their violence."

"But they maintain order that way, don't they? They keep us safe?"

"Do they? What about Lucian? Is he safe? You're only safe if you fall in line and salute, and even then, it doesn't last long," Rump replied.

Rump took a look at my dazed face and sighed. "Let's head back to Eileen."

Placing his arms around my shoulders, we walked down the corridor towards the control room.

CHAPTER 10
THE MASSACRE

"Somebody do something! Why are we standing here watching them die? We've got to help them! They're being slaughtered!"—Erik

"There's our bright boy and look, he's made a friend," Ginger said, taking a jab at me. "Aren't they a precious pair?"

"Don't mind him," Rump ordered, standing in the doorway to the control room, where Tumor and Ginger were monitoring the flickering screens. "Ginger always has a case of the ass."

"Looky here people, I'm a busy man. I don't have time for a love-in right now," Ginger said, giving Rump a pointed glance.

"You wouldn't know a love-in if you landed in the middle of one," Rump replied with a grin. "Erik, this lunatic talks tough, but he's solid gold through and through. Stick close to him and keep your eyes open."

"What am I—a babysitter now?" Ginger called out to Rump as he walked off into the compound. "Obviously, I have nothing better to do than play nursemaid to a newbie," he muttered as he turned his back on me and returned his attention to the wall of flickering screens.

"Look, Eileen told me to meet her here," I explained. "I don't need a babysitter and I definitely don't need you on my back. Just pretend like I'm not here."

"Done," Ginger replied dismissively, moving closer to one of the screens. "Tumor, I need a close-up on Quadrant 4 pronto."

Tumor isolated a section of the screens and zoomed in just as a series of explosions rocked the quadrant, where a throng of protesters had gathered. Many of them were carrying wooden sticks with signs affixed.

Some read "Freedom Now!" Others: "The Revolution Is Here!" And still others read: "Fight Back. Resist!"

Caught off-guard by the blast and the resulting mayhem, the protesters scrambled for cover, but there was nowhere to go. They were surrounded by an army of metallic, skeletal androids equipped with lasers who were firing into the crowd.

People were screaming, attempting to flee, trampling each other in their terror. One woman, holding a small child, was struck by a laser beam that severed the back of her blouse, setting her afire. The force of the blast sent her flying face-first into the hot, searing pavement, smoke spiraling above and over her. Blood dotted the clothes of the protesters who surrounded her.

Another, an old, emaciated bearded man, was attempting to escape when a robofly landed on his back. With its sharp metallic teeth, it tore a plug of bleeding flesh from his neck.

"Isn't somebody going to do something?" I asked. "They're being slaughtered! Why are you standing here watching them die?"

"There's a time for fighting and there's a time for watching," Ginger replied with a growl. "There's nothing we can do for those poor fools anymore. But this is your first lesson in survival if you're planning to last more than a day underground: better think before you act or you'll wind up getting your brains blown out while the robos keep on killing."

"Ginger's right, Erik," Eileen said, having arrived in time to see all hell break loose. "We've got to pick our battles and this isn't it."

The carnage continued.

A man with shoulder-length hair, probably in his mid-twenties, with blood running down his cheek was holding a sign that read: "Peace." One of the androids lifted him by his neck and slowly choked him to death. His limp corpse fell to the pavement with a thud.

"This is a massacre!" I muttered, unable to look away.

A Raptor 9 robotic dinosaur smashed a dozen or so lean-tos and tents. Those inside began screaming. Blood was seeping into the debris as human hands and feet peeped from beneath the tents.

"This horror show isn't going to end anytime soon," Eileen said, dragging me away from the horrors on the monitors, away from the control room, and towards the bunking area with its bank of lockers. "It's time to go topside. If we can help Lucian while we're up top, or at least find out where he is and what's happened to him, all the better. But we can't go unprepared and defenseless."

"What have you got?" I asked, watching her rummage through a locker.

"This, for starters," she said, as she turned with a magic bullet like the one she used to open the digital locks. "It's a neutralizer that creates a temporary lapse in the technology that maintains the locking devices. It can temporarily freeze temporal lobe chips. It was designed by Spidus. Here," Eileen said, as she handed me my own personal magic bullet. "Just press this button on the blunt end and it will activate."

"Got it," I said as I pocketed the magic bullet.

"I'm sure you've seen these before," she said as she handed me a pistol-type object. "It's a Resat. It will administer an electronic shot to a victim and momentarily incapacitate them."

"These are illegal," I said, staring at the outlawed device in my hand.

"You've already broken so many laws by now, one more won't make a difference," she said. "And this one might save your life."

"I get it," I said, my eyes trained on whatever other contraband Eileen had stashed in that locker.

"That's it for now. Ginger can show you a few other things when the time is right," she said. "This will help with our little surveillance project."

"Where exactly are we headed?" I asked.

"We need to go topside. F-Zone. That's where the Violence Reduction Centers are," Eileen replied. "We know Lucian was being taken to one. We'll track him from there."

"Do you think we might be in time to save Lucian?"

"One can only hope," she answered with a doubtful smile. "But we've at least got to try. Either way, we need more intel on what they're planning."

"I feel like I'm in a dream I can't escape."

"This dream is a nightmare," she said. She hesitated for a moment, then grabbed my hand and squeezed it companionably. "Come on. Let's roll."

CHAPTER 11
CHILDREN OF THE SUN

"Your intestines are writhing like a frightened worm, and your belly button is gyrating like a tenuous UFO in a dark, vanilla sky. It makes me want to sink my little pearls into your belly and rip your guts out."—The Neon Snake

"So what's the plan, exactly?" I asked Eileen, trying to appear as matter-of-fact as she was about the fact that we were planning an excursion into enemy territory.

"The plan is for you to keep your eyes peeled, your lips zipped, and your hero impulses in check," Ginger muttered as he joined us.

"Wait. He's coming with us?" I asked.

"Only as far as the entrance to the underground tunnels," Eileen explained. "Ginger knows those tunnels better than almost anyone else."

"But I thought we were going topside?" I asked.

"Let that be a lesson to you to leave the thinking to the grown-ups," Ginger responded with a wide grin, only to grimace when Eileen punched him in the arm.

"Ginger knows a shortcut to the Violence Reduction Center where we think they're holding Lucian," Eileen explained. "The shortcut takes us further underground and brings us out under the Center. But we've got to go topside to find the right entrance."

"Eileen will make it through just fine. I'm not sure how the Mole People will feel about Boy Wonder here, though," Ginger said, another provoking grin inching over his face. "They may not let him pass."

"He'll pass," Eileen said, not breaking stride. We were moving into a narrow passageway now. I hurried to keep pace with her, leaving Ginger to fall behind us.

"Explain," I demanded, looking at Eileen. "I need to know what we're going up against."

"The shortcut goes through underground tunnels burrowed centuries ago by the Amraks—a.k.a. the Mole People—the creatures who inhabit the inner Earth."

"You're serious?" I asked, a slight grin forming. "This isn't some rite-of-passage prank on the new recruit?"

"I'm dead serious," Eileen replied. "The Amraks don't trust Topsiders and have steered clear of humans for centuries. They do not look kindly on anyone who ventures into their territory. Most never make it out alive."

"And Ginger knows this shortcut, how?" I asked.

Before Eileen could answer, Ginger piped up, "Listen, Wonder Boy, that's intel that gets shared on a need-to-know basis. Right now, all you need to know is that Eileen is in charge."

"What about you? Aren't you coming with us?"

"I've got better things to do than babysit you two," he retorted, coming to a stop at an unmarked door that looked as if it hadn't been breached in decades. "Eileen knows the drill, and she knows the markers that will lead you to the tunnels."

Looking at Eileen, Ginger nodded, some imperceptible message seeming to flow from one to the other. "You meet up with trouble, you know what to do," he murmured as he opened up a disguised panel in the wall. Punching in a series of codes, Ginger glanced over at us. "You'll have three minutes to exit through this door and find the entrance."

"Wait," I interrupted. "Where does this lead? What happens if we don't find the entrance?"

"Then you're out of luck," Ginger said, wrenching the door open, shoving us through and shutting it behind us.

We were in a round cavern of some kind, with high-ish ceilings, crumbling brick walls, and roughly a dozen doorways ringing the perimeter of the room. Each doorway was set into an elaborately carved frame embedded with strange symbols and figures.

"Where are we?" I asked. "I thought we were going topside."

"We are topside—or as close to topside as we need to get," Eileen replied from across the room, running her hands along door frames and peering at the carvings over each doorway. "We've been walking on an upward slope the whole time. You just didn't notice. Like our highways, these tunnels connect the Amrak civilization which exists at the center of the earth. Just beyond one of these doors is a passageway that brings you out into a cavern beneath the lake at Central Park."

"What are we supposed to do—swim our way out?" I asked.

"Not this time," she answered, with a quick look at her watch. "We need to find the tunnel that leads to the Amraks. It's behind the door marked with the Cheshire Cat's smirk. And we need to find it fast."

"What happens if we don't find it?"

"If we don't find it before the timer reactivates the door locks, then we'll be stuck here for a while with no way in or out again. And Lucian will be lost for good."

"Tell me what to look for," I said, straining to make sense of the strange carvings around the doorways.

"Big cat, big cat fangs, crazy cat smile," she said, moving on to the next doorway.

I moved in the opposite direction, scanning doorway after doorway for something that resembled a cat. There were carvings resembling robots, snakes, elephants, even some kind of three-headed hydra, but so far, no crazy cat. Our time was running out.

Eileen and I converged on the last door at the same time, pointing simultaneously to the top corner where a smiling, demonic cat's face loomed over the doorway with the fangs of a vampire.

Grabbing hold of the doorway, I tugged it open and prepared to launch myself through it only to have Eileen pull me back. "Lesson 1: look before you leap."

Before us lay a chasm fathoms deep and pitch black. Had I stepped blindly through the doorway, I would have been a goner.

"Lesson 2," I muttered. "Let the lady lead."

Eileen reached beyond the doorway and pulled out a rope that was tied to the inside of the frame.

"Here, hold this rope," Eileen instructed. "We have to descend for a while in a downward rope climb. We made a deal not to build or construct anything in the tunnels, including stairwells."

"That's why we're climbing down a rope?" I asked.

"Yeah. An agreement with the Amraks. We're allowed to traverse the upper caverns without notice as long as we do no damage," she said, reaching into her backpack and pulling out her Resat, which she clipped onto her belt loop.

"And the laser is for what, exactly?" I asked.

"The Amraks tolerate us, but they're not exactly welcoming," she explained, hoisting herself through the doorway and onto the rope. "The laser will serve as a warning in case anyone tries to get in our way."

Pulling out the laser she'd given me, I echoed her movements, attaching it to my belt loop so that it dangled in reach of my hands.

"I'll descend first, and once I'm down 50 or 60 feet, I'll give a yell," Eileen instructed. "Then you start letting yourself down. It's about a 20-minute climb to the cavern floor, and we'll be on our way."

"Be careful," I said. "I'll be right behind you."

"Be sure to pull the door closed behind you," Eileen said. She started easing herself down into what looked like a dark coal tunnel that entered the earth at a slope. She was quickly enveloped in darkness.

"Okay, Erik! Time to fall down another wormhole."

"I'm game. Here I come!" I called back, swinging onto the rope and pulling the door shut behind me. With my feet firmly planted on the tunnel walls, I began my downward descent into another realm.

As I let myself down the rope, inch by inch, slow minute by slow minute surrounded by an interminable darkness, my jaw began to twitch. My eyes began to water like crazy and whirring images started cascading before my eyes.

I went into a dream of sorts, although it felt like a nightmare. Bats started circling my head: little fiends with bright red eyes and faces as demonic as the Cheshire cat up top. Something grabbed and tightened around my waist.

Startled, I almost let go. I strained to see what had me in its clutches. Reaching for the laser, I flicked the switch so its light cut through the darkness only to yell and almost lose my grip on the rope again.

A large neon snake was coiling around my midsection. As its head came eye level with mine, its cavernous mouth opened to rows of sharp teeth and a large, glowing, red tongue emerged. My head bolted back as the serpent spoke in a giggling, high-pitched voice. "Your intestines are writhing like a frightened worm, and your belly button is gyrating like a tenuous UFO in a dark, vanilla sky," the serpent hissed and continued. "It makes me want to sink my little pearls into your belly and rip your guts out."

"Eileen!" I screamed.

The snake whispered, "I get under your skin, do I? Well, keep your wits about you and maybe soon, I'll pay you another visit, maybe next time for dinner."

"Eileen, something's wrong!" I screamed. "Help!"

"Here, Erik," Eileen said as she grabbed my foot. Almost immediately, the snake unwound itself from my waist and slithered over me, disappearing into the darkness above. "Let yourself down easy."

"Quick," I said, leaping away from the rope and onto firm ground. "We've got to get away from here. It's not safe ... There are monsters!"

"There are monsters all around," she said, "But these particular monsters are in your head."

"No, this was a huge snake. It had me in a death grip," I gasped, still shaken and reeling from the brief encounter.

"I'm sorry. I should have warned you that the descent into Amrak makes your imagination run wild," Eileen said, her hand on my shoulder. "It's the mushrooms that grow on the walls of the caverns."

Stopping, she leaned forward, plucked something from the cave wall, and showed it to me in the palm of her hand. It was a strange red mushroom with yellow spots dotting its surface. "These are psychedelics.

Ingest them and you're on a different plane of existence for days. The aroma alone will send you tripping."

"I could have done without that particular trip," I said, cocking an eye at her.

"You'd better toughen up, then, because that's nothing compared to what lies ahead," she said, sounding irritated and moving towards a glimmer of light in the distance. "If Ginger is right, this should lead us to the entrance to where they're holding Lucian."

"Lead on," I said as I followed Eileen's dark outline toward a dim, distant light.

After a couple hundred yards, Eileen came to a sudden stop. "Wait. Who's that?"

I stepped to her side and there, in front of us, maybe 50, 60 feet ahead, was the outline of a tall, thin creature with a large head.

"We are with Spidus," Eileen said loudly as her words echoed around us. "We are here to help a fellow comrade—my brother—who has been captured by the Controllers. We need access to a Violence Reduction Center whose entrance may be up ahead. Can we pass?"

The creature slowly lifted one hand. It had three slender fingers and spoke in a robotic voice. "I have your mind print. I've analyzed it. You can pass," the creature responded. He turned and pointed at me. "I have concerns about your traveling companion, however. His mind has not completed realignment yet. Be on your guard. He could revert to his former state."

"Thank you," Eileen responded, holding her hand in a similar position, a greeting of some sorts, I suppose.

As we drew closer to the creature, its features became clearer. Large, deep-set, sparkling hazel eyes with long, fine blonde hair hanging down over its shoulders. Its mouth was small and its lips pursed as it spoke. "You will want to turn here. Access to the facility that you mentioned is only a short walk beyond the perimeter. Stop at the luminous, metallic stairs. The stairs are used by those commanded by the Controllers. They are humanoids that work and cooperate with the Greys. We have become aware of a plot by the Greys and certain elements of your race to cojoin forces—inner and outer earth creatures—and rule the entire planet." Then stopping as if it were computing, the creature continued, again as if it were a robot. "You will not have very much time at your destination. The room you will enter is a storage unit, but it is used when agents of the Controllers descend into the earth. They traverse it frequently."

"Are you Enki?" Eileen asked.

"Yes, and you are?" the creature responded.

"I've heard of you. Glad we have met. I am Eileen and this is Erik. We work with Spidus."

"Ah, Eileen. Yes, you are known. We are of one mind with Spidus. He understands the Children of the Sun, our ancestors. We know his intentions and they are laudatory."

"We feel the same," Eileen said. "Thank you for allowing us to pass and for your guidance."

"Our pleasure," Enki said as he stared unnervingly, unblinkingly into my eyes.

Eileen nudged me with her foot.

"Ahhh … thank you, Enki," I said, following her lead. "You've been a big help."

"Growth comes with pain, and it awaits you on your journey."

"Okay," I said, puzzled as Enki's hazel eyes drilled into me. I could literally feel my thoughts being pulled from my head into his. I was being analyzed like a bug under a microscope.

"We need to move," Eileen directed. "We're losing time."

"I'm ready," I said, nodding goodbye to the tall one.

We turned and headed into the darkness of the tunnel. "We shouldn't have much further to go," she said. "Look for the glowing stairs."

Up ahead, a set of stairs rimmed in lights beckoned us onward.

CHAPTER 12
BATTLEFIELD OF
THE DEAD

"Let's leave this hell to the monsters who created it. We've got some thinking to do."—Erik

I tried to imagine what lurked in that room at the top of the stairs. Gruesome images winged their way through my mind like demon bats on the hunt. Still nothing I could have dreamed up would have prepared me for what awaited us.

"Wait," I called to Eileen in a quiet whisper. "Are we playing into their hands? Aren't they expecting the Resistance to try to infiltrate their outposts?"

"They'll be looking for us to come straight at them. They're not going to expect us to come in the back door from an underground cavern. At least, I hope not. It's our only chance to try to get to Lucian before they turn him."

I was starting to have my doubts that we'd make it in time to save Lucian, but I kept those feelings to myself.

"I'll go up first," Eileen whispered. She was little more than a faint outline in the subterranean darkness. "Follow close behind, Erik."

"I'm right behind you."

I looked up at a set of poorly lit, ancient steel stairs that scaled several landings. As we climbed, the stairs shifted and swayed, groaning in protest the higher we ascended.

We came to a stop on a small platform outside a nondescript door.

Eileen reached in her pocket for her magic bullet. "I can disable the cameras and the other sensors in the room we'll be emerging into, but it will be temporary."

She waved her magic bullet at the sensors on the front of the door and I heard the familiar click. Pausing, she turned and stared intently at me. "Your job is to watch and learn, and jump when I say jump. Otherwise, no heroics. Understood?"

"Yes, ma'am. At your service."

Eileen signaled for me to follow her. "Silence until I speak. Here we go."

She opened the door to a dimly lit room.

The room seemed to be a makeshift storage space lined with shelves stocked with various size boxes. The air reeked of rotting meat. Leaning forward, I peered at the boxes. One was labeled "Synthetic Gauze." Another read "Hypodermic Needles." Yet another "Laser Scalpels."

I was about to gag from the stink when Eileen motioned me over to another small door. "One more lock and we should be in," she whispered. "Hopefully, I can disable the surveillance cameras and sensors long enough for us to get a handle on where Lucian might be. If we can get him out, that's the priority. Otherwise, we just gather intel and get out."

Again, the magic bullet worked its magic: the door lock yielded with a quiet click and we gained entry to the room beyond.

Eileen gently eased the door open to a room that was brightly lit but stank of death and decay. I covered my nose and mouth and tried hard not to retch while Eileen took a digital reading of the air.

"The camera and sensors are temporarily disabled, but the air is filled with high doses of toxic chemicals, so we can't stay too long," she said. Moving towards an open doorway, Eileen stepped into a large room lit by flickering, buzzing fluorescent lights. "Oh God!"

Hurrying into the room, I moved alongside her, only to reel back in disgust.

"What is this place?" I asked.

Before us was an ocean of beds with rows of what appeared to be dead bodies lying across them. Some were covered in green sheets. Some were fully exposed with either their heads or extremities hanging off the beds.

"Hurry," Eileen commanded, passing a small pen camera to me. "We need to make sure Lucian is not among these bodies. Try to gather some photographic intel for the boys back at the lab while you're looking for Lucian."

I pointed the camera at a naked man lying face up on one of the beds, his life's blood dripping to the floor. His genitals had been surgically removed, but crudely so. There was also a grizzly canyon where his eyes had been, now empty sockets, blood oozing out of them.

Eileen turned away from the gruesome tableau only to jump back in horror. I found it hard not to lose the contents of my stomach then and there. Lying before us was the body of a human being, but where its head should have been, a reptile's head—as if from a large lizard, snake-type eyes and elongated tongue gaping from its multi-teeth mouth—had been neatly sewn or stapled in place. Blood, dark burgundy colored, oozed from the incisions. The body bore a close resemblance to Lucian.

Nothing in my life topside had prepared me for this kind of butchery. Moving closer to the body, I peered at the inside of its left arm. Lucian had a noticeable scar that ran from the underside of his elbow to his wrist.

With a sigh of relief, I stepped back and shook my head at Eileen. Whoever this poor man was, it wasn't Lucian.

I stepped around the reptile man's bed to the next row of corpses and pulled down a green sheet covering another dead body. This one was child-like, however. On the death pallet was a small gray creature about three feet tall with a large head. Its eyes were wide open, large and black, like two infinite pits of doom.

Out of the corner of my eye, I caught a glimpse of something moving a few beds over, slowly twitching under a green sheet on one of the deathbeds. I turned and slowly walked towards it, stopping to look over my shoulder at Eileen. She motioned me forward.

With each body we uncovered, there was a building dread that we'd find Lucian butchered, mangled or turned into a freak experiment.

Once again, I held my breath, dreading what I'd find, hoping against hope that Lucian had been spared this fate.

Stepping to the side of one bed, I slowly pulled the sheet down, exposing some violently twitching eyes. Pulling the sheet further down, I exposed the rest of the face. My eyes wanted to turn away from the horror, but something urged me forward.

It was a human face—a man's face, although not Lucian's—but the lips had been removed, much like the corpse's genitals had been. The man's eyes were dark slits in his bloodied, bruised face. Blood was everywhere. He seemed to be trying to speak, but I could barely understand what he was saying.

"Help me!" he rasped, blood gurgling in his throat and shooting out of his mouth.

The effort to speak took all he had left in him. With a gasping breath, his chest heaved, his eyelids closed and he dropped off into nowhere.

I'd had enough.

I covered the corpse with the sheet, turned and did a quick survey of the remaining corpses. "Lucian's not in this tomb of horrors, thank God," I murmured. "Wherever they've taken him, let's hope he fares better than these poor souls!"

CHAPTER 13
PARADISE LOST

"We humans are good at taking what we need but we're not very good at giving back."—Eileen

It felt as if we descended those rickety metal stairs and walked through the tunnel in half the time it had taken us to traverse them the first time. Both of us were on high alert, driven by the need to get as far away from that foul chamber of death as quickly as possible.

We walked in silence, both of us wrestling with our private demons.

At the mouth of the vertical tunnel where we would begin our upward climb, Eileen paused. "It's hard to believe looking at it, but this used to be the entrance to a paradise."

"This place?" I asked, looking around the dark, musty tunnel.

"At one time, this tunnel and others led to lush forests, animals of every kind, even dragons, humanoids of different varieties, waterways, streams and rivers filled with clean water and wildlife."

"So what happened?"

She shrugged. "What always happens. When the Topsiders used up all of their resources, they started to invade other realms. Paradise didn't stand a chance against the strip mining and the excavating and the fracking. We humans are good at taking what we need but we're not very good at giving back. So the Amraks retreated further into their inner earth sanctums. And when the Topsiders had leached everything good they could find down here, they abandoned it in search of other realms."

"Has anyone ever breached the Amraks' inner sanctums and lived to tell about it?"

"Spidus has," she replied. Before she could say anything more, a faint clatter broke the still silence of the tunnel. Whether it was near or far was hard to say as sound traveled strangely in the tunnels, but it was enough to send us scurrying up the rope.

The upward climb was less eventful than our descent, thankfully. Although the psychedelic mushrooms made us feel as if we were free floating through time and space, we made the climb without encountering anymore talking snakes.

Reaching the top soon after Eileen, I secured the rope to the inside of the tunnel entrance and helped Eileen re-engage the locks.

We couldn't re-enter Subterranea the same way we'd exited, so we had to navigate through a maze of old subway tunnels until we could find one that would lead us topside and into my old stomping grounds.

Emerging into the open air, I squinted against the watery natural light, the first I'd seen in some time. Eileen slipped on a pair of eye visors and handed a pair to me. "These will shield your eyes from the biometric sensors. They emit a signal that baffles the facial recognition cameras," she murmured, her lips barely moving. "Be careful what you say while we're topside, though. The cameras are everywhere and they can read your lips."

I figured we'd have to make our way back to that old junk shop in order to get back to Subterranea, but Eileen led me through the teeming streets to a back alley crowded with trash cans, piles of discarded boxes and a stench that made my eyes water.

Approaching a dumpster covered in filth, I noticed an old guy dressed in rags, sitting with his back against it. He appeared to be sleeping, but when we neared him, he raised his eyes, studied us briefly, offered us a glimmer of a smile, then slumped forward and began snoring loudly.

Something about the encounter seemed to reassure Eileen that it was safe to proceed, because she motioned for me to follow her behind the dumpster. Hidden by its bulk from passing eyes and aerial spies, she used her magic bullet to open a small door, low to the ground, at the rear of the dumpster where a garbage chute would be connected. We shimmied our way into a secret crawl space barely big enough for the two of us. Eileen waited until the door had re-sealed behind us before keying in a complicated sequence into a hidden panel buried on the false floor of the dumpster. Suddenly, the floor below us dropped away and we went into a free-fall.

I grabbed for Eileen as we tumbled out of the dumpster, only to land on a tarp that sprang closed around us like a cage and lowered us slowly to the ground.

Eileen and I were so tangled up in each other, it took a moment to realize that the tarp had opened up and dropped away from us. Still on high alert, I used my body to shield her from whatever new menace awaited us.

"Isn't this romantic?" a mocking voice drawled. "We send out a search party for Lucian, and what do we get back? Two lovebirds. How sweet."

"Shut it, Ginger," Eileen grumbled.

I breathed a sigh of relief. Ginger wasn't my idea of a welcome party, but he was better than the alternative.

As my eyes got used to the artificial light again, I focused in on Ginger, leaning back in a metal chair and drinking some sort of canned brew. We had landed in a small chamber with no visible entrance or exit except for the trapdoor in the ceiling that connected to the dumpster.

"Well, well, look what the cat dragged in," Ginger said, eyes narrowed as he watched us disentangle ourselves. "No Lucian, then?"

"Not at that Reduction Center," Eileen said, brushing remnants of the dumpster off her arms and legs. "They're using it as a dumping ground for Ravenscragg's pet projects."

"That was a morgue for failed experiments, not a conversion center," I added. "Those people died painful deaths."

"One more lesson in reality, Wonder Boy," Ginger shrugged as he pulled out his communicator and began keying in a series of codes that caused a panel in the wall to open up. "Sometimes it takes pain to wake you up to the facts of life."

I took a deep breath and resisted the urge to wipe the smirk off Ginger's face with a punch to the nose.

"Enough, Ginger!" Eileen growled, stepping through the panel and glancing back at us. "Remember, it's the Controllers who are the enemy."

"Enemies come in all shapes and sizes, baby," Ginger offered up with a big grin that showcased his pointed incisors. At Eileen's glare, he held his hands up in surrender. "Hey, can I help it if I'm a realist?"

"Maybe the world needs a few more dreamers," I said hotly, following Eileen out of the chamber and putting some distance between me and Ginger.

"Maybe you're right," Ginger said, a thoughtful look in his eyes as he stepped through the opening and re-sealed the panel. Turning back to Eileen, he said, "Spidus wants a debriefing before you do anything else. Afterwards, I'm heading topside for Mattie's get-together if you two want to come along. Might be a good idea for the Dreamer, here, to meet some of the Wonderland gang."

Eileen was already nodding in agreement as they moved down yet another passageway. I followed, completely lost in this underground maze.

"Perhaps they can help get the word out through the network about Lucian," Eileen said. "We could use more eyes and ears on the ground to find out where he is and what they've done to him."

"Mattie's got rats in all corners of the kingdom, so that shouldn't be a hardship," Ginger replied.

"Who is this Mattie anyhow?" I asked.

"Mattie has worked with the Resistance for years. She started off as one of Spidus' protégés," Eileen said. "She took Ginger in after he escaped from the Werewolves. Brought him to F-Zone."

"So she's on our side?" I asked.

"Mattie stopped taking sides a long time ago," Ginger responded with a side glance at Eileen.

Eileen sighed. "Like just about everyone in the Resistance, Mattie has had to develop her own coping skills to survive. She's known as the Mad Hatter. Her heart is solid gold, but she has a bit of a temper."

"And she doesn't tolerate fools," added Ginger.

"What Ginger means is that she's become very unstable, so tread with caution around her," Eileen emphasized. "When you meet her, just smile and bow your head. Don't look her straight in the eye unless she invites you to do so. She hates that. And don't be thrown by her appearance."

"Why? What's wrong with her?" I asked.

"Nothing's wrong with her," Ginger muttered. "Look, I've got things to do. You head to the debriefing on your own. I'll meet you at the stairwell in Q quadrant at 6 pm sharp."

Eileen waited until we were alone again to explain. "Mattie's wiring went haywire at some point during her work with the Resistance. I don't know a lot of the details, but she lives by her own code now."

"I still don't get it."

"Mattie has been known to carry a torch and wear a crown of thorns," Eileen said. "She won't hesitate to kill. She's severed the heads of a few rogues who dared to challenge her. She actually took one guy's head and carried it on a spike through the streets of F-Zone, blood dripping and all."

"She sounds like a perfect hostess to me." I said.

"Just stick close, Erik, and you'll be fine. Keep your mouth shut unless spoken to by her," Eileen instructed. "And whatever you do, don't eat or drink anything while you're at this gathering."

"Right," I said. "No eye contact, no speaking unless spoken to, no food or drink, and no inciting the hostess to madness and mayhem. Anything else?"

"A shower wouldn't hurt," Eileen said, wrinkling her nose as she paused outside Spidus' quarters. "Spidus might wish he had waited for his debriefing. We smell like we just crawled out of a dumpster."

I sniffed the air around us. "You know, I'm kind of getting used to the smell. It smells like insurrection."

CHAPTER 14
THE CATHEDRAL

"Yeah, kid, if you want to float on the ship of fools, you gotta follow their rules."—Ginger

We were on our way to Mattie Hattie's so-called tea party.

We'd arranged to meet after the Spidus debriefing in yet another strange chamber connected to the main underground headquarters by a series of twisting and turning passageways.

I was completely disoriented.

Ginger led us down even more desolate-looking channels until we arrived at a heavy, nondescript metal door with no distinguishing features other than a strange set of marks scratched across the surface. Ginger used his magic bullet to unlock the door, which opened onto a small room barely big enough to serve as the landing for a spiral staircase that soared several stories high.

For the second time that day, I embarked on what felt like an interminable climb that ended only after my calf muscles had begun screaming for relief.

Waiting until all three of us were crowded onto a small, hatched platform connecting the floating staircase to the wall, Ginger pulled out what can only be described as a magic wand and pointed it at the small digital light above the door.

The door slowly creaked open.

"Showtime!" Ginger proclaimed, pulling a weather-beaten, crumpled top hat out of an inner coat pocket and setting it on his head at a jaunty angle. "It's a date! We can't be late!" he yelled as he charged through the door, brandishing his magic wand over his head. The room glowed with an orange, pulsating light. "No time to ruminate, oscillate, obfuscate, or calibrate. It's eight, my mate! Conflate!"

"What's up with Ginger?" I whispered to Eileen, taken aback by the sudden—giddy—transformation that had come over him.

"He may have had one too many pieces of happy candy in preparation for Mattie's tea party," Eileen whispered in reply.

"Happy candy?"

Eileen shrugged, watching Ginger dance ahead of us in the orange-filtered light with a twinkle-toed step.

"Can he be trusted to lead us in the state he's in?" I asked, glancing at Ginger, who had stopped in front of a small, three-foot high door, dropped down on all fours, barked like a dog, and pushed the door open. It swung open to virtual darkness.

"Time to crawl through the tunnel, my friends!" Ginger announced as he squeezed his way through the miniature doorway.

Eileen smiled, the first real smile I'd seen cross her face. "He's harmless in this state, but he's not completely senseless. He won't let us come to harm."

I shrugged my shoulders in bemusement, then signaled for Eileen to enter. She got down on all fours, and I did the same, as we followed Twinkle Toes into a small, dark tunnel.

"Just a few more minutes, and we'll be in F-Zone," Ginger said, as his magic wand slapped the floor here and there while he crawled forward with Eileen and me trailing behind him.

Finally, Ginger stopped at a place where the ceiling rose high enough to allow us to stand up. He was breathing hard. He slid a round metal cover to the side above him. It clanked as a burst of light shot into our eyes. Ginger's torso, then his legs disappeared as he pulled himself up through the round opening.

I boosted Eileen up so Ginger could help her ascend, then I followed suit.

Pulling myself up through the hole, I crawled onto sharp gravel that cut at my hands and knees. Straightening up, I looked around to find that we were standing before a building with a tall steeple.

"Time for church," Ginger said.

"Seriously?" I turned to Eileen. "This is why I climbed a million stairs, crawled through a mile of dank tunnels, and sliced up my hands and knees—to attend a church service?"

Eileen gave me THAT look, the one that said I was being an A-1 jerk.

"You, my boy, are used to people congregating on the neural network to worship a state-sanctioned God," Ginger declared. "What you're about to experience is old-time religion! Get ready for a transcendent experience!"

"Transcendent or not, stick close and keep your eyes peeled," Eileen added. "Any type of gathering will draw the wrath of the Atlas Fours, the roboflies and their buddies, not to mention a few other members of the robotic opposition."

"Wonder Boy, you're in for a treat!" Ginger waved his wand at me. "Let's go in and see if the party has begun!"

As we walked up the stairs leading into the building, the double doors that served as the entrance suddenly swung open. Before us was a bald-headed man with tattooed swirls covering a scarred face, dressed in black leather pants, a vest over a bare chest and large, jagged earrings.

Stepping out, he proclaimed in a voice that sounded like a snake hissing, "Very good. My favorite spice has arrived for the festivities. Good to see you, Ginger!"

"Scar, it's been awhile," Ginger said, gesturing towards Eileen and me. "I've brought Maid Marion and her boy wonder, Erik!"

"Welcome to Wonderland," Scar hissed with a grin that exposed his dark, metal-capped teeth. They looked as if they had been ground to a point like sharks' teeth.

I took a step back only to have Scar grab my arm and drag me towards him until his face was about six inches from mine.

"Only my friends call me Scar, of course," he hissed, opening his mouth and shooting forth his tongue. It was long, split down the middle and wiggled like two snakes tied together. Spittle flew all over my face. "You can call me Sir Scar."

I flinched. "Of course. I wouldn't presume to be so presumptuous ... uh, Sir Scar," I added hastily as he frowned menacingly at me.

"Good," Scar hissed as he turned and walked through the double doors.

"Scar was caught and interrogated by a Werewolf Unit. Before he escaped, they tortured him, trying to get him to speak," Eileen said as I wiped Scar's spittle off my face. "They sliced his tongue and carved up his face. Thus, the name Scar."

"Enough shilly-shallying and dilly-dallying," Ginger said in a sing-song tone. "We mustn't be late."

"We're right behind you," Eileen answered.

Ginger stepped forward and through the large double doors. We followed him into an ancient cathedral littered with rows of wooden benches facing a wooden stage and adorned with the boarded-up remnants of stained glass windows that glowed from small patches of outside light.

"Oh, my, look who's joining us," Ginger said in a hushed tone. He stopped and cut his eyes to the right. "The Iceman cometh!"

Turning, I saw a tall old man approaching, long white hair falling over his shoulders and his face half-hidden by a long white beard. His body was covered in a blue robe that glittered and sparkled. His hand was holding a long walking stick that he pounded on the floor with each step he took.

"Your majesty, it's so good to see you," Ginger said, slightly bowing his head.

"You're so full of crap, Ginger, that I don't know how you breathe," the Iceman said. His voice was so hoarse I didn't know how he was getting the words out of his mouth.

"Takes one to know one," Ginger replied with a demon smile.

"Then you must be one," the Iceman rasped, followed with a childlike giggle.

"Iceman, you know Wendy. This is her lost boy, Erik, but he's no Peter Pan," Ginger said, reaching out and shaking hands with our new acquaintance. "Erik is on trial until we see what he's made of."

"Glad to meet you, boy," the Iceman said with a laser-eyed stare. He bowed his head to Eileen and then surveyed the room. "Is it party time?"

"Soon, my friend, soon," Ginger replied. "I hear some of the guests approaching."

As the old man shuffled away, I leaned towards Eileen. "What's his story?" I asked, nodding at Iceman's retreating back.

"Another victim of the Controllers' torture tactics," Eileen said. "The Werewolves packed him in a coffin filled with ice as a punishment, but he survived."

"What kind of punishment is that?"

"A brutal one, but he didn't break," Eileen replied. She glanced away, a far-away look in her eyes that suggested she was thinking of Lucian and what methods the Controllers might be using to "break" him.

"Lucian won't break. He's a survivor, too." I wasn't sure if I was trying to reassure Eileen or myself, though.

She didn't agree or disagree. She just smiled sadly. "By the time they pulled Iceman out of the coffin, the water in his skin cells had started to form ice crystals and his skin had turned hard and white. He was eventually picked up by Spidus and the boys. He's been the Iceman ever since."

"Looks like Red Riding Hood is already here with Wolfen," Ginger interrupted, pointing to the stage.

A grown woman in a red, hooded outfit stood talking to a guy dressed in a black tuxedo and shirt whose face was covered with dark, matted hair.

"You've got to be kidding," I said in disbelief.

"I wouldn't kid a kid," Ginger retorted, waving his finger at my face. "You're too big a joke to kid about."

"Time to sip some tea. Let's go!" Ginger declared abruptly as he turned and started high-stepping again.

Eileen tugged at my hand and moved toward the stage.

"Come on, Erik. It's time for you to meet some of the elite of F-Zone's resistance movement," she said.

Ginger stopped, turned and looked back at me. "If you want to float on the ship of fools, you gotta follow all their rules," he chortled with a toothy grin. "It takes someone out of step with the crowd to resist the Controllers, and these folks don't mind their manners, they don't tolerate fools, and they sure don't play by the ruler's rules."

"Any fool can make a rule, and any fool will mind it," I retorted.

"He's quoting the pencil-maker!" Ginger declared as he spun on one foot and turned, leading us towards the stage, his wand waving in the air. "If you've got Thoreau in your repertoire, there may be hope for you yet, Kid Galahad."

CHAPTER 15
MATTIE HATTER

"That's Elizabeth Batthori. The Controllers tried to alter her DNA by exposing her to some sort of electromagnetic stimulation. It worked, kind of, but it turned her into a blood-sucker."—Eileen

A long table with twelve chairs was positioned on either side of the stage. A large throne sat at the end of the table. To the far right of the stage stood a giant wooden cross.

Standing before the cross, with his back to us, was a guy sporting long brown hair and a beard who appeared to be contemplating the cross, standing as still as a statue.

We walked up a small set of stairs that led to the stage and paused behind the guy communing with the cross.

"What's his deal?" I whispered into Eileen's ear.

"That's JC," Eileen said. "He's new to Mattie's gang. Werewolves tried to crucify him—pierced his hands and feet and stuck a crown of barbed wire on his head. He doesn't move too far from that cross. Lives here in the building and sleeps behind the stage."

"CLUMP! CLUMP!" came the crashing noise of Iceman's staff as it pounded the wooden stage.

Ginger and Scar took up positions on either side of the throne.

"Let the party begin! Let us gather together!" Ginger announced as a motley crew filtered in from behind the stage and sat at the table.

"We will need two extra chairs today," Ginger directed. A tall, bald guy grabbed two folding chairs and placed them on the floor on the opposite end of the table, facing the throne.

"That's the Eggman," Eileen said, cutting her eyes toward the bald guy.

"Silence!" Ginger proclaimed. "Prepare yourselves. Mattie Hatter is on the move!"

Everyone stood. Eileen elbowed me in the side and nodded her head toward the throne.

I jumped to attention. The silence was shattered by the Iceman's staff pounding the stage.

"The tea party will commence," Ginger announced. "James Hook, will you please do the honors?"

Hook, dressed in a long red waistcoat topped with a large hat, stood up and started playing a flute. The noise was so off-key, it pierced my ears.

As the noise invaded the air around us, a large, bird-feathered bonnet glided towards the stage. Beneath the bonnet was an elongated woman's head. Her large, pointed nose poked the air in front of her. Eileen leaned towards me and whispered, "Whatever you do, do not make eye contact with her."

I nodded and watched out of the corner of my eye as the mysterious Mattie Hatter slowly made her way to the front of the throne, a flaming torch held high in her hand.

Mattie cleared her throat and began to speak in a whispery murmur. "'Will you walk into my parlor?' said the spider to the fly. 'Tis the prettiest little parlor that ever you did spy.'"

As one, the gathered throng responded, "We will, your Majesty!"

"In that case, welcome to my web," replied Mattie. "Sit, comrades, and let us begin the strategy session. As usual, there is no tea today. But for those seeking the Way, there is always the wafer and the wine." Mattie then threw off her headdress and long, sparkling black outer garments to reveal a frail woman dressed in rags. Circling her head was a crown of thorns.

"The feast is prepared," Ginger said with a wave of his wand. "Lizzie, will you do the honors?"

"Sure enough, Gingie!" Lizzie, a large woman in a long black dress, a knife attached to a belt around her middle, began to distribute small goblets to the attendees.

"Good stuff, Mattie," remarked a man of middling height with a face covered in white paste. His mouth was painted bright red.

"Glad you like it, Bela," Mattie replied graciously, raising her goblet. "We do make great raisin wine."

"Blood's better, but we do what we must." Bela smiled just wide enough that a pair of fangs glinted between his bright red lips.

Mattie glared at him. "And where are our delicious wafers, Bela?"

"Ah, yes, the wafers," Bela stuttered, offering up a large, tattered jewelry box.

Faint music sounded as Bela opened the box and pulled out a bag of wafers, handing it to Wolfen, who passed it down the line until it reached Mattie.

Reaching into the bag, Mattie pulled out a thin wafer of dark chocolate and placed it in her mouth. "Very tasty," she said, passing the bag back to Wolfen, indicating that he should take a piece of the candy and pass it on down the line. Everyone partook except for Eileen and me.

Just then, a man entered the room, dragging his leg behind him and carrying a tall slender plant encased in a golden pot.

"The tree of life!" Mattie exclaimed. "Give Butcher a hand." She gestured to Scar and Wolfen to help Butcher set the tall plant down in the middle of the table.

"Maid Marian, you have brought a stranger into our midst," Mattie declared. "Introductions are in order, are they not?" Although Mattie directed her question at Eileen, she stared fixedly at me, a maniacal gleam in her beady eyes.

"Your Majesty, Erik is a new recruit," Eileen explained. "He is a friend of Lucian's. Spidus is handling his training personally."

Mattie studied me for a moment in silence.

"Present yourself!" she barked.

I glanced at Eileen who was tugging at me. "Now what?"

"You're supposed to present yourself, Erik," Eileen whispered, shoving me towards Mattie's throne. "Remember: don't look her in the eye."

"At your service, your Majesty!" I said, bowing my head with a sidelong glance at Ginger, who nodded approvingly.

"Twinkle twinkle little bat, how I wonder where you're at, up above the world you fly, like a tea tray in the sky," Mattie declared, placing her right hand on my shoulder and waving her left hand over my head in some form of benediction or blessing. "Welcome to the Rat Pack, my little rodent dropping."

"Uh, thank you, your Majesty," I murmured as the entire party broke forth with insane, screeching laughter.

"You can drop the formality now that we're acquainted," she said with a girlish giggle and a bat of her eyes. "To my friends, I'm just plain ol' Mattie Hatter."

"Thank you, Mattie," Eileen said, moving forward and grabbing my arm.

"Yes, thank you, Mattie," I echoed.

"Beat it now," Ginger said, pointing his wand at us and directing us back towards our chairs.

Sitting down, I surveyed the table again. The one called Lizzie looked like she was drinking from a human skull.

Eileen followed my gaze. "That's Elizabeth Batthori," she said. "The Controllers tried to alter her DNA by exposing her to some sort of electromagnetic stimulation. It worked, kind of, but it turned her into a blood-sucker."

Before I could formulate a reply to that startling bit of news, Scar stepped in front of the throne. "Atlas Fours and Raptors have been spotted approaching the front door. Time to run," he hissed. "Run!"

"Follow me, my fellow inmates," Mattie yelled, waving her hand and pointing behind her throne.

Pulling back the red curtains behind Mattie's throne, Scar and Ginger ushered us backstage. Mattie led the way. Eileen and I trailed behind the procession.

Scar and Ginger scurried by us with Ginger waving his wand over his head. They positioned themselves on either side of Mattie. "Move quickly.

The robos should be coming through the doors at any moment," Ginger said, looking over his shoulder at us.

Loud crashing noises sounded behind us as the machines smashed through the walls and invaded the room.

"Something or someone was tracked here," Ginger grumbled as he and Scar stared at me accusingly.

Before I could respond, someone yelled out.

I turned and there, clenched in the jaws of a 7-foot robotic Raptor, was James Hook,

"Not Jamie!" Mattie cried out.

"Damnit!" Ginger growled. "We can't risk a rescue!"

I don't know what came over me, but I sprang away from Eileen, leapt through the curtains and off the stage, crashing onto the floor below. Now on all fours, I stared that iron lizard right in the eyes. It was chewing on Hook's neck. His blood dripped to the floor. He was done for.

Grabbing a chair, I charged the metal beast, smashing it across its midsection. It took a swipe at me with its iron claw, dropping Hook's limp body to the floor with a thud. Ducking, again hitting the floor, I slid behind the beast.

"Erik!"

Looking up, I saw Eileen on her knees at the edge of the stage. "Run!" she screamed.

The Raptor turned its head towards me, emitting a shrill metallic shriek.

"Chew on this!" I screamed, grabbing the discarded golden plant pot—someone had had the foresight to yank the plant out and take it with them—and hurling it into the beast's jaws, which clamped onto it and jammed.

I had temporarily disabled its lethal overbite, but its talons and powerful legs could still slice and crush.

Turning, I ran for a side door. Behind me, I could hear the Raptor's clanking feet crashing against the floor as it came after me. My heart was about to come out of my chest when I lunged at the door, smashing it to the ground.

Light shot forth into the room as the brown, stinking, polluted air rushed into my nostrils. On one knee, I turned to see the Raptor's lower body through the door opening. I spun around, ran around the corner, and headed for the back of the building.

I ran for my life.

CHAPTER 16
THE FLAW IN THE FLUE

"We live to fight another day."—Ginger

"You knucklehead!" Ginger snarled as he grabbed me by the arm and pulled me through a side entrance of the cathedral.

"You can yell at me later," I gasped, trying to catch my breath.

"That's a promise," Ginger replied tersely, already on the move. "Let's get going!"

Ginger bounded up a small flight of stairs with me in hot pursuit. Pushing back some tall curtains, we stepped into a backstage area, where the rest of Mattie's party had gathered to hide.

"Hook didn't make it out, but Boy Wonder here managed to distract the enemy enough to temporarily scramble their programming," Ginger announced to the assembled group. "The machines are circling the front of the building, so we'd better scatter fast."

"Erik!" Eileen couldn't seem to decide whether to hug me or hit me, so she did both.

"Tut tut, Maid Marian, that's no way to treat a hero," Mattie admonished, as several "bravos" rang out from the small throng. "A true act of chivalry," Mattie said. "You are worthy."

"Worthy of what?" I asked, looking Mattie straight in the eyes for a moment before quickly lowering my own.

"Worthy of your prize," Mattie replied loftily, taking Eileen's hand and placing it in my own.

"Your Majesty, the award ceremony will have to wait," Ginger advised. "We can't afford any more casualties."

Mattie nodded regally in agreement, gathered up her skirts and began to hustle her troops towards their escape route. "Let's get on down the road, my fellow rats. Keep your heads on and your hearts on fire."

"We'd better follow suit," Ginger ordered, gesturing to me and Eileen.

Racing out the back door, we followed Ginger into the twilight of F-Zone. "Head this way. Try to get lost in the crowd. Maintain a visual trace on each other, but don't appear to be traveling together. Whatever you do—" he said, looking straight at me, "—don't attract attention by playing superhero. You're outnumbered out here. The goal is to make it back to Subterranea in one piece. Now move."

"Here, Erik," Eileen said, running her magic bullet over my forehead. "This will deactivate your chip a little longer."

"Just don't deactivate his brain, Eileen," Ginger sneered. "He's going to need what little he has to get out of this alive."

"Would you stop riding me, already?" I snarled back.

"Better me than that E-bot turning the corner," Ginger said, pointing to a small three-foot creature headed toward us.

"Their laser blasts will cripple you," Eileen said. "Forget trying to blend in. Run for it!"

Ginger wheeled and started down the street, his wand flying out of his hands, spiraling up in the air and landing on the ground. There was no time to stop. He kept going.

I swept up the stupid wand with one hand and with the other, grabbed Eileen's hand as we trailed after Ginger. Just then, a laser beam blast screamed over our heads and hit the side of the building. Glass and wood shot up into the air and smashed to the ground.

"Take cover up ahead!" Ginger yelled over his shoulder. "Pick up the pace!"

Eileen pulled ahead until she was running alongside Ginger. "C'mon, Erik," she yelled, looking back at me.

"Doin' my best," I replied, half out of breath as I heard the E-bot shift into flight mode. We were out of luck. There was no way to escape once that thing was in aerial pursuit.

"Flip that wand over here!" Ginger yelled, coming to a standstill about 50 feet away from me.

"Are you nuts?" I screamed. "You still have a chance. Run!"

"Toss it!" Ginger ordered. "Now!"

Looking back at the stinging machine, which was now airborne and closing in fast, I tossed Ginger his wand and sprinted towards him.

In one smooth motion, Ginger dropped to his knees, pointed the wand at the hovering E-bot, and shot forth a laser blast that knocked the E-bot off-kilter.

Before it could recover, Ginger blasted it again.

The flying robot teetered in the air, choked, and then crashed to the ground with a thump.

"I owe you one, man," I gasped as I stumbled to a halt next to Ginger.

"Just don't make a habit of having me save your neck," Ginger said, pushing himself up off the ground. "That was payback for what you did for Hook. Now we're even."

"If you two are done slobbering all over each other, you might want to take a look at what's moving towards us," Eileen muttered.

Crisscrossing up ahead, three skeletal androids were rapidly moving back and forth across the street. Their metallic skulls flinched spasmodically while their bright blue eyes scanned the terrain.

"They're on the prowl," Ginger said. Suddenly, a loud scream pierced the air as one of the droids snatched a young woman off the ground and started carrying her away.

"Time to motivate down the road, people," Ginger said.

"Wait, we can't just let them take her," I protested. "She's done nothing wrong."

"Not our battle," Ginger muttered, ducking down a narrow alleyway between two buildings.

"C'mon, Erik," Eileen urged. "They'll let her go once they realize she's not part of the Resistance. But we can't afford to get caught. There are too many lives depending on us now, Lucian included."

With one last look behind me, I followed Eileen down the alleyway. Turning left at the end of one of the buildings, we hurried across a park littered with garbage and building debris.

Strewn among the discarded trash were discarded people of all shapes, sizes, colors and ages: the down-and-out and forgotten elements of F-zone. Some of the homeless were rolled up in newspapers or rags, sleeping on the ground. Several had set up makeshift campsites with fires burning over small wood logs. Pots and pans were strewn here and there.

Ginger waited impatiently for us at the edge of the small park. Pointing to a narrow, upright building standing on the edge of the field, he said, "That's our ticket out of here, if our luck holds."

"I think you spoke too soon," I muttered as another scream pierced the air.

Appearing out of nowhere, one of the skeletal robots was moving quickly across the field, carrying a weapon of some sort. Homeless people scurried out of its way. One woman grabbed a little girl up in her arms and ran for cover.

"Hit the ground!" Ginger screamed, shoving Eileen and me down and leapfrogging over us, attempting to use his own body as a shield.

Before I could do much more than drag Ginger under a pile of trash, scant protection from the lethal beams that screeched as they passed overhead, a familiar voice hissed out a warning. "Time to return to the junkheap, you piece of crap!"

"It's Scar!" Eileen said, peering around my shoulder.

"Take this home to momma, you heap of junk!" Scar hooted as he fired a cobbled-together, junkyard rifle from his hip. It hit the android square on the chest and exploded on contact. Sparks and small lightning bolts shot forth from the android's head. The metal beast fell forward onto the littered grass with a thud.

"See, you thought I was good for nothing." Scar helped us to our feet.

"You're too good," Eileen said, reaching up to kiss Scar's mottled cheek.

"We live to fight another day," Ginger said, shaking off some of the debris that was clinging to him and slapping Scar on the back.

Scar nodded and started to walk away. "Gotta go and make sure Her Majesty is safe. You troublemakers need to stop picnicking and get outta here. Those metal beasts usually travel in packs."

"Scar," I called out. "Thank you."

He lifted an eyebrow in acknowledgment. "The difficulty is not so great to die for a friend as to find a friend worth dying for," he said.

"You know Homer?" I asked with a note of surprise I couldn't quite disguise.

"I know a lot of things, bird brain," said Scar. "All you need to know right now is how to keep your head down, your lips zipped and your mind open. I can't be expected to save your sorry hides every time you run into trouble." With a twitch of his head, Scar turned and loped off across the park.

"Third time had better be the charm," Eileen said. "Let's get out of here while we can."

With Ginger taking the lead, we walked up to the small rectangular building he had pointed out earlier. A sign hung over tattered, ancient elevator doors. Barely visible, tarnished gray letters proclaimed it the Brooklyn Subway.

Eileen waved her magic bullet at the digital pad located to the left of the doors. With a creek and a crash, the door slid open to reveal a dark stairway.

"You know, Scar isn't the only literary member of the Resistance," Ginger said, punching me lightly on the arm as we began our descent back to Subterranea. "I personally find Ogden Nash is more my style …"

"A flea and a fly in a flue
Were imprisoned, so what could they do?
Said the fly, 'let us flee!'
'Let us fly!' said the flea.
So they flew through a flaw in the flue."

CHAPTER 17
LUCIAN'S EYES

"The system is run by those who view us as cattle on the way to the slaughterhouse. And the Controllers certainly don't want the cows to revolt. They want us to serve their needs and then walk peacefully to the gallows."—Spidus

"Smells like something died down here," I exclaimed as we ventured deeper into the bowels of the old Brooklyn Subway.

"Give the boy a prize," Ginger replied as his laser light illuminated a stairwell that was littered with human skeletons, some with rotting flesh still on their bones. Rats, feasting on the carcasses, skittered away from the ghostly light.

"Were they running to something or away from something, I wonder?" I asked, taking a quick mental count of the number of bodies ... six, seven, eight ... all of them frozen in agonized contortions.

"Whatever caused their deaths—it was something they encountered down here—and we don't need to be its next victims," Eileen said in a strangled voice. "We need to get out of here right now!"

Stepping warily over and around the skeletons, we made our way down the stairs. At the bottom, we arrived at a set of heavy, sealed double elevator doors. A purplish sliver of light gleamed through the crack between the doors.

"Is this the only way down from here?" Eileen asked, examining the door for any signs of recent activity.

"Unless we want to go prowling in search of another stairwell or try our luck topside again, this is our best bet," Ginger replied. "We'll ride this down to its last stop, then navigate the tunnels by foot."

Pursing her lips resolutely, Eileen waved her magic bullet. We braced as the doors creaked slowly open, prepared to flee or fight. Stepping forward into the purple haze of the elevator's cubicle, Ginger gave the all-clear and motioned us forward. Eileen once again used her magic bullet to override the elevator's internal controls and propel us down to the lowest level.

The doors closed slowly behind us. Just before they shut completely, a small, dark shadow darted past the narrowed opening.

"What was that?" I asked.

"Whatever it is, you'd better be grateful that it's out there and we're in here," Ginger replied. "Let's just hope there's no welcoming committee waiting on the other end of this line for us."

The tense silence was broken only by the groaning box as it traveled deeper into the earth. After a few minutes, the elevator ground to a halt. As the doors opened, Ginger aimed his wand at the widening crevice.

We braced for a surprise attack, but for the moment at least, we were all alone. Exiting the elevator into a dim cavern, we cautiously patrolled the perimeters of the space—Ginger taking the lead—until we arrived at a series of five portals, each leading to a separate tunnel.

The tunnels all looked alike to me, except for one that emitted a strange, humming light. This was the tunnel that Ginger started down. We followed, senses on alert for any sounds that might indicate an ambush.

We walked in silence in the strange, humming light. The tunnel twisted and turned but sloped steadily downward all the while, until we came to a dead stop at a place where the ceiling had caved in and blocked the passageway.

"Now what?" I asked, worn out and hungry. "There's no way we're going to be able to shift that pile of rocks. We'd better head back and see if we can't find another way around."

"Don't give up so easily, Boy Wonder," Ginger said as Eileen walked a few feet away from us, back the way we had come, pulled out her magic bullet and began running it from one side of the tunnel wall to the other, starting at the ground and moving upwards.

"What's she doing?" I asked.

"I'm creating a sealed force field so we'll know if anyone attempts to follow us," she explained with a quick glance over her shoulder.

"Follow us where?" I asked. "We're at a dead end."

"Tut tut," Ginger said mockingly. "Haven't you learned that things are not always what they seem?"

"Well, this *seems* like the end of the road," I retorted. "Unless that wand of yours can make these rocks disappear."

"Nah, we don't need my wand," said Ginger. "Don't you have your own magic bullet?"

"Yeah," I said, pulling out the device Eileen had given me earlier.

"Activate it," Ginger ordered.

I pressed the small button on the blunt end as Eileen had done. Nothing happened.

"One more time," Ginger instructed, "but this time, point it towards that small gray rock in the corner."

Once more, I activated the magic bullet, pointing it towards a small, smooth pebble the size of a gumball.

Suddenly the pitch of the humming light that had filled the tunnel changed and the rocks began to morph before our eyes.

By the time Eileen rejoined us, the unpassable pile of rocks had reconfigured themselves into a doorway, beyond which was a metal door inset with an electronic pad similar to the ones I had seen Eileen deactivating earlier.

At a nod from Eileen, I waved the magic bullet once again, breathing a sigh of relief as the door opened and we found ourselves back in Subterranea.

"Ginger, what took you so long, man? The boss needs your presence pronto, dude," said a small, elfin man guarding the entryway. "He's in the Control Room."

"On my way, Cornelius," Ginger said. "Anything I need to know?"

"You're to bring these two with you," Cornelius said, giving me a squinty-eyed stare.

Rolling his shoulders and cracking his neck, Ginger led us through another maze of passageways until we arrived back at the Control Room. On the screens, some talking head was providing a recap of the day's news while footage of the skeleton androids attacking us flashed behind him.

"Hey, that's us!" I said, pointing to the screens.

"Look at that, Sherlock! You're famous!" Ginger smirked. "You're in for it now."

"Hey man!" someone yelled at us from the side. It was Tumor. "Spidus has been asking for you!"

"Yeah, yeah. Keep a lid on it. We're on our way," Ginger said, shooting a sidelong glance at Tumor as he ushered us past the entrance to Spidus' enclave.

Spidus lay on his bed at the far end of the room, looking up at a screen. Standing behind him was a large, surly, burly guard holding a rifle.

"You can beat it now," Ginger said gruffly to the armed man.

"Okay, Spidus?" the guard asked, speaking in a deep southern twang.

"Yes. Thanks for your help, Duke," Spidus said in a groggy voice, still staring up at the screen.

Glancing up to see what had captured his attention, I stepped closer to the screen plastered on the wall. "It's Lucian!"

Eileen rushed over for a closer look.

"His eyes," she murmured, pointing at the screen, her finger quivering just a bit.

Studying Lucian's eyes, my head bolted back on my shoulders. "His eyes used to be gray, like Eileen's. They're like black coal now. What did they do to him?"

"He's been reprogrammed," Ginger answered. "Rewired."

"How?" I asked, looking at Spidus for confirmation.

"Most likely through a prefrontal lobotomy or an electromagnetic manipulation of certain parts of his brain," Spidus said with a tired sigh. "The eyes—the window to the soul—always give them away."

"But reprogrammed to do what?" I asked incredulously, glancing over at Eileen.

"He'll probably be used as an assassin of sorts for the Controllers," Ginger speculated, moving closer to the screen to peer into Lucian's face.

"But Lucian doesn't believe in violence," I muttered, looking up at Lucian's face. "None of this makes any sense."

"That's not Lucian anymore," Eileen said in a broken tone.

"Eileen is right, boy," Spidus said in a gentle tone. "What you're looking at—that face up there—is no longer human. It's the face of a machine that exists only to serve the Controllers now."

"They destroy everything good and decent," Eileen remarked bitterly, her voice beginning to break.

"Not everything," Spidus reminded her. "They haven't destroyed you. Or Ginger. Or Rump. Or Erik. Or the Resistance."

"Lucian used to be in that list," she said, looking up at the screen.

"I don't know what will happen to Lucian, or if the things that make him the Lucian we love—courage, compassion, decency—can survive the butchers and the mad scientists and the torture teams," Spidus said slowly.

Eileen's eyes welled up with tears. She turned her face away from us.

"What are they trying to achieve?" I said, trying hard to blink back the tears in my own eyes.

"We're dealing with an enemy that has lost its humanity and wants power at all costs," Spidus replied, his tired old eyes fused with mine. "Life on this crazy, malfunctioning planet is a question with no satisfactory answer, but for Lucian's sake, we need to keep asking those questions," Spidus said, slowly sitting up in his bed.

"Nothing makes sense," I muttered.

"If you really think about the pain we inflict on one another and the pain we suffer from birth to death, no, nothing makes sense. People getting beaten to a pulp. Massacred. Tortured. Enslaved. Imprisoned." Spidus shrugged. "Most of these people have done nothing wrong, but in the Controllers' crazed world, innocence and guilt make no difference. In the end, we're all treated the same."

My eyes were riveted to the screen, watching Lucian's empty, dead eyes. "Why don't people fight back then?"

"Why didn't you fight back, Wonder Boy?" Ginger said, with a gleam in his eye. "For the same reason no one else does: you've been taught to obey."

"Most people are just trying to get by," Eileen said, coming to stand beside me. "Just trying to stay alive."

"It's not much of a life, of course, but when it's all you've got, you'll still fight to hold onto it," added Spidus. "And of course, the Controllers have done a good job indoctrinating people to believe if they just obey the government and do what they're told, everything will be okay."

"But everything is not okay," I muttered.

"No, everything is not okay," Spidus agreed. "We've been sold a lie. Freedom is a lie. We're not free. We're slaves."

"Slaves in bondage to monsters." I drew a ragged breath, remembering some of the more painful lessons I had learned the few times I dared to speak up or step out of line.

"I get that we're slaves," I said. "I get that we need to break free. But what are we going to do to help Lucian?"

"Lucian is beyond our reach now," Spidus said, grief etched on his aged face.

"I don't believe that," I countered. "I refuse to believe that." I looked to Eileen, but she turned her eyes away.

"Refusing to face up to reality is the fastest way to end up dead," Ginger warned.

"Please," I said, turning to Spidus. "Lucian's my friend."

"To help Lucian, you must find the answer to the question," replied Spidus in a hoarse whisper, his eyes beginning to close.

"What is the question?"

"That is for you to find out. Only when you know what question to ask and then seek the answer to that question will you be able to save Lucian from himself."

CHAPTER 18
THE RATLINES

"The Nazi leadership had a well-developed plan of escape when it looked like their center of power—Germany at the time—seemed to be collapsing. They established ratlines, which were secret routes spread across the world that allowed the key Nazi leaders and scientists to escape. Their escape was aided and abetted by those who were supposedly at war with the Nazis. The world powers did not want Nazi science and technology to go to waste."—Edgar

It was dark. I was exhausted. My mind was reeling.

The slender bunk mattress provided no comfort to my weary bones. The darkness provided no respite from the horror-laced images racing through my mind.

I didn't want to be alone with my thoughts.

I didn't want to be alone. Period.

"Eileen, you awake?" I whispered into the darkness, which was broken only by the low, glowing lights on the ceiling.

"Hard to sleep after a day like today," she whispered back.

I shifted onto my side so I was facing her.

From the creaking of her cot mattress, I could hear her doing the same.

"Nothing seems real anymore," I muttered.

"Pain is real," an all-too-familiar voice rumbled into my ear. I shot off the bunk and into a fighting stance.

"At ease, Wonder Boy," Ginger murmured. "Save the heroics for when they're needed."

Eileen eased into a sitting position on the side of her bunk, her head cocked sideways, and stared up at Ginger. "What gives?"

"The Werewolf Units are at it again," Ginger grunted, plopping himself down on the edge of Eileen's bunk. "They just raided a college dorm. Your dorm, I believe," he said, nodding in my direction.

"Was anyone hurt?" I asked.

Ginger shrugged. "When the Werewolves are involved, it's a sure bet there will be fatalities. Their usual M.O. involves smashing, maiming and killing."

"What was the casualty count?" Eileen asked, glancing over at me.

"We're still waiting on further intel," Ginger replied guardedly, glancing sideways at Eileen. "A few students. At least one was part of the Resistance."

"Who was it?" I asked, thinking of the few friends I had among the college crowd.

Before Ginger could respond, we were interrupted by a tall, thin guy with a large protruding belly hanging over his belt and a gray pallor typical of someone who hadn't seen the sun in a while. "Spidus wants you."

"Thanks, Gut," Eileen replied. "We're on our way."

We entered Spidus' cave single file, with Eileen in the lead. Ginger and I followed.

"What is Edgar Alan Johnson doing here?" Eileen asked, glancing back at Ginger.

"Edgar who?" I asked.

"Edgar Alan Johnson," Ginger replied, nodding in the direction of a tall, thin man, his face gaunt and gray, standing near Spidus' bed. "He's our resident historian. One of Spidus' inner circle."

Johnson, dressed in a brown, pin-striped suit, white shirt and dark tie, and clutching an old, tattered collection of papers, watched us approach. Thin, wire-rimmed glasses hung down his nose.

"Edgar, this is the young man who found the manuscript," Spidus murmured.

"Pleased to make your acquaintance," Edgar said in a curious British accent, every word pronounced slowly and articulately. "Shall I begin, Spidus?"

"A few explanations may be in order, first," Spidus replied, glancing briefly at the omnipresent screens before turning his attention back to us.

"Yes, of course," Edgar replied stiffly.

"The Controllers are growing stronger and more aggressive," Spidus said. "There are some indications that they've hacked into all of our systems now. We're doing all we can to block them. Even if we do, they've most likely gobbled up a lot of our most sensitive info."

"What does that mean for the Resistance?" Eileen asked.

"It means we don't have much time to fight back," Spidus said, his eyes at half-mast.

"Is it even possible to fight back when they've got all the advantages in terms of weapons, technology and manpower?" I asked.

Spidus opened his eyes and looked straight at me. "That's when you must fight the hardest and the smartest."

"You're talking about strategy," I said.

"Strategy, yes," he nodded. "But even more important than strategy is heart. You have to want it badly enough."

"But what if—" I started to ask, only to have Eileen elbow me gently in the side.

I took the hint and waited for Spidus to continue.

"There's a third essential ingredient, just as important as strategy and heart," he rasped, "and that is knowledge. Edgar will give you a bit of background on what we are facing and why."

Edgar steepled his fingers under his chin. "Approximately a century and a half ago, a Deep State elite made up of financiers, politicians, military generals, and surveillance overlords from each of the industrialized countries came together in secretive meetings to form the Third Reich. The word Reich meaning order or empire. In attempting to resurrect the old Roman Empire, they reinvented it as a police state run by Nazis."

"Sure, they were headed up by the guy with the mustache," I responded.

"Adolf Hitler," Eileen clarified.

"And do you know what happened to the Nazis?" Edgar asked, now in full instruction mode.

"They were wiped out in the war," I responded.

"That would be too easy, don't you think?" Ginger prodded.

"Ginger is correct," Spidus interjected. "That kind of evil doesn't just go away."

"No, it does not," agreed Edgar. "The Nazi leadership had a well-developed plan of escape when it looked like their seat of power in Germany seemed to be collapsing. They established ratlines, which were secret routes spread across the world that allowed the key Nazi leaders and scientists to escape."

"Didn't anyone try to stop them?" I asked.

"Stop them?" Ginger snorted. "Who do you think helped them escape?"

"Their escape was aided and abetted by those who were supposedly at war with the Nazis," Edgar explained. "The world powers did not want Nazi science and technology to go to waste."

"So where did they go?" I asked.

Edgar grimaced. "They moved into positions of influence and leadership all over the world, including here. With their expertise, the Nazi brain trust was welcomed by those who had a vision—"

"—a nightmare vision—" inserted Ginger.

—of creating a total control society. In this way, the Third Reich kept its manifesto alive and expanded its sphere of influence."

"How could people not have known better?" I sputtered, aghast.

"When have people ever known better?" Ginger muttered, lounging against a small table littered with scraps of paper.

"The Nazis were skilled at manipulating and controlling the masses through the use of psy-ops programs." Edgar clutched his tattered book tightly.

"They still are," Eileen murmured.

"It's a con game," Ginger snarled.

Spidus nodded in agreement.

"The Nazis used the schools and Hitler Youth groups to indoctrinate the masses," Edgar continued. "In this way, they became quite adept at spreading their disease of compliance and depersonalization down to the masses subliminally."

"Today, the Controllers use mass media, screen devices, and brain chips as the vehicles for indoctrination and control," Spidus added.

Eileen looked at me pointedly. "The few that resist and think for themselves end up in concentration camps or living as outlaws in F-zone or Subterranea."

"So what if we destroy their communications centers?" I asked. "Disable the signal they're using to control people?"

"It's an interesting idea, Erik, and one we're pursuing," Spidus said with a nod in Ginger's direction, "but the evil empire's reach goes far deeper now."

Edgar cleared his throat and resumed his lecture. "The Nazis developed crude prototypes of much of what we see today in terms of flying androids and robots. Even the crude medical procedures you've seen practiced on resistors were developed by the Nazi medical experts and scientists."

"You're talking about what we saw at the Violence Reduction Center," I said.

Edgar nodded. "The inhumane experiments have continued. Organ removals, head transplants and so on."

"What's the point?" I asked. "An army of ghouls?"

"Ding, ding, ding. Give the boy a prize," huffed Ginger, picking dirt out from under his fingernails.

"An army of ghouls is exactly what they're after," Spidus said. "They want a master race of fiends that will be so all-powerful that any resistance will be futile."

"The detention camps are also a critical part of the Controllers' plan for total domination," Edgar added.

"There's one located right outside of F-zone," I said, recalling all the times I had passed it without much notice.

"That's one of the worst ones, too," said Eileen.

Edgar sighed wearily. "These prisons house hundreds and in some places thousands of inmates who slave up to 12 or 14 hours a day to create the electronic devices the Controllers use to track and control the populace, as well as the weapons they use to keep the people in line."

"So if we infiltrated the prisons, we could undermine the technology. Booby trap it or something," I said.

Ginger stopped picking at his nails and glanced over at me with a glimmer of approval. "Not bad, Boy Wonder."

Spidus remained silent.

Eileen reached over and grabbed my hand.

CHAPTER 19
THE RED ROOM

"So as we've discovered, the only way we can make any headway is to covertly undermine them by lying, cheating, stealing, and trying to make better gadgets than them. It will mean causing havoc on their technology and jamming their networks."—Ziggie

"Erik, we're dealing with some very sick people who view us only as expendable items of consumption on the food chain," Spidus said. "But we don't have to give up. We can fight this. We may lose, but fight it we must. That's just one of the many reasons we must mount our counteroffensive and soon."

"I want to help," I said.

"We are grateful for your help—and your heart," said Spidus. "Time is running out for the Resistance to bring about any significant change."

"I need to do something. I want to help," I repeated.

"Each of us has a part to play, you included." Spidus leaned forward. "Remember: Strategy. Heart. Knowledge." On the last word, he collapsed back onto his bed, eyes closed.

"That's my cue," Ginger interjected. "Let's go powwow, Boy Wonder. Spidus needs to rest."

Spidus managed a tired smiled as Edgar leaned in to whisper in his ear.

Eileen and I followed Ginger, who was talking rapidly into his handheld device.

"There's a war session going in the Red Room," Ginger said, glancing back at us. "You're invited." He turned and started walking quickly in the direction of the Red Room. Eileen and I trailed behind him.

There was no idle chatter. We were all lost in our own thoughts. I couldn't conceive of how to go about defeating something so evil.

Skirting around an office divider, we entered a space dominated by a bright red, triangular table. Three people sat at the table: a man and woman on one side, and an old guy with a shaved head and neatly trimmed beard to their left.

Eileen carried out the introductions, starting with the bearded guy. "Erik, this is Ziggie. He works with our destabilization unit. These two are his coworkers Ruby and Ken."

Ruby, dressed in a tight-fitting, black, synthetic leather suit that wound itself up and under her chin, nodded a greeting. Ken stared straight ahead.

"Spidus wants us to take preemptive action and soon," Ginger said, slouched next to Ruby, who batted her eyelashes invitingly at him.

"It's too soon," Ziggie said, typing frantically into his hand-held. "We need more time. There's still so much we don't know."

"We're running out of time," Ginger said. "They've been sending out more and more sweeps into F-zone to round up resistors."

"We need something big," muttered Ruby. Ken remained silent, staring straight ahead.

"They've got Lucian," Eileen added. "If they manage to break him, they'll know everything we've been working on, including the location of all of our cells and the identities of the members of the Resistance."

"Something flashy and big," muttered Ruby.

"Why not blow up one of their control centers?" I suggested.

"Sounds like you've been watching too many action flicks, Wonder Boy." Ginger tipped his chair back. "Unless, of course, you're volunteering for a suicide mission ..."

"They have the robotoids, the ammo and technology to wipe out a full-scale army," Ziggie explained. "We'd be outmanned, outgunned, and outmaneuvered before we even had a chance to start."

"Blowin' stuff up ain't goin' to work, kid," Ruby rasped. "I was trained in the martial arts and I went up against their heavily armed cops and look what it got me." Standing, she placed her foot on the edge of the table and rolled her pant leg up. Her lower leg was a metal, artificial limb that glittered in the light.

"Ruby learned the hard way that violence doesn't work," Ken piped up quietly.

"They also took a souvenir from me," she said, holding her hand out. Three of her five fingers were gone. Severed. Only the index finger and thumb remained. "They definitely have my DNA now," she said with a grimace.

"The Controllers and their minions thrive on pain and violence," said Ziggie. "They are energized by violent acts. It charges their batteries."

"So if you can't beat them at their own game, then what's left?" I asked, glancing around the table.

"The only way we can make any headway is to covertly undermine them by lying, cheating, stealing, trying to make better gadgets than them," Ziggie responded. "It will mean causing havoc on their surveillance technology and jamming their networks."

"We've been somewhat effective in causing some commotion in their systems. That's one reason they're preparing to target us for elimination," Ken added. "But we need some better intel before we can take any more decisive actions."

"You're talking about infiltrating their network," Eileen said, leaning in.

"Our plan is to infiltrate the central power source of the enemy," Ken explained. "It's where most of the key decisions are made. It's where the Controllers meet, roundtable and strategize. That's where the Hive Mind originates. It's where the Queen resides and runs the show."

"The Queen?" I asked.

"Yes. The Queen of Hive Mind," Ruby said. "The Topsiders and, to a certain extent, the rest of us are all affected by the Hive Mind."

"It's like an insect empire run by the Controllers," Ken emphasized. "As in nature, or what's left of it, the queen bee controls the hive."

"Why not send me?" Ginger suggested.

"We can't spare you, Ginger," Ziggie said. "Spidus will want you to stay close."

"I can do it," Eileen volunteered. "Count me in."

"It will be dangerous," Ken warned.

"I can handle it," Eileen insisted.

"She has a good track record," Ginger chimed in. "And she was able to snatch Erik before they nabbed him."

"Count me in, too," I said.

Ginger started to say something, shook his head and shrugged.

"Alright, Eileen and Erik it is," Ziggie confirmed, getting nods from the other three. "The Queen Bee's Hive is located in a secured, underground palace. We have a bead on the Hive and where it's located. We need intel on its internal operations."

"You two will have to enter it from a topside entrance," instructed Ruby.

"We've been working on something that might help you gain access," said Ken. "Gordon, are you near?"

"I am indeed." I turned to see a man approaching us, dressed in a black suit, white shirt and a red bowtie. "Gordon Novel at your service."

"Escort Eileen and Erik to the Molecular Destabilization Unit," Ruby ordered.

Gordon gave a smart salute and beckoned us over.

"Microwave Man will take it from here," Ruby said, dismissing us. "Try to come back in one piece."

CHAPTER 20
THE MOLECULAR
DESTABILIZER

"We are a rather sloppily directed video game but with a little action and lots of pain thrown in as a bonus or, should I say, as a way of keeping us from diverting from the path they've planned out for us."—Microwave Man

Gordon led us to a midsized room lined with screens. A grouping of tables took up most of the room, covered with all types of electronic equipment. At the very center of the grouping of tables was an old wooden desk covered with glass cylinders. Effervescent, light green liquid welled up in the tubes.

With a flourish, Gordon pulled out a chair for Eileen. I pulled up a chair alongside her, grateful for a chance to rest my tired legs.

The room's only occupant was a middle-aged man dressed in a t-shirt, blue jeans and sporting a short goatee. On his head was a metal cooking pot, handles on both sides.

Looking up, the man smiled congenially. "Welcome," he said. "I'm Frank Olsen."

"Otherwise known as Microwave Man," Gordon interjected.

"Unfortunately, that is my handle," Frank acknowledged.

"Why is that?" I asked.

Frank grimaced. "As a young recruit to the Resistance, I was captured by Werewolves. They tried to force me to divulge as much information as possible about the movement. I gave them what I knew, which wasn't much and certainly not damaging to the Resistance, but they didn't believe me."

Tears welled up in Frank's eyes.

Eileen reached over and patted his hand. "The Werewolves used electrical shocks to persuade him to talk."

"The pain was indescribable." Frank shuddered. "But by the time they were done with me and had returned me topside, I had a new talent, thanks to them."

"One of the unseen byproducts of the torture is that it led to Frank's ability to pick up their rays in his head," Gordon explained.

Frank shrugged dismissively, his eyebrows raising a bit on his partially exposed forehead.

"The Resistance couldn't do without you or your talent," Eileen said.

"Yes, well…" Frank blushed crimson all over.

"Let's get started, shall we?" Gordon cut in.

"Right. Rump and I have come up with a way for you two to penetrate the Hive, collect information and, hopefully, return safely here," Frank explained.

"You work with Rump?" I said.

"We work together in developing whatever makeshift technology we can come up with to divert the ELF rays from penetrating our skulls." At my questioning look, Frank expounded, "ELF is an acronym for the electronically low frequency microwaves that bombard us from everywhere. Thus, the aluminum pot on my head. It's proving very effective in deflecting those damn rays."

Frank shook his head, causing the pot to rattle. "ELF rays can induce a hypnotic-type state as they penetrate the cranium but without the targets knowing that their minds have been infiltrated. They can also contain mental suggestions. That's how the Controllers induce compliance and control the masses."

"Yeah, Rump told me about the invading rays from the screen devices and cell towers," I replied.

"It can be a dangerous weapon in the hands of those who use it," Gordon interjected.

"We are a rather sloppily directed video game but with a little action and lots of pain thrown in as a way of keeping us from diverting from the path they've planned out for us," Frank opined. "It's all in your DNA, which acts as an antenna broadcasting your genetic information into the systems that compose or make up your digital pattern."

"So it's all a game?" I asked. "We're just playing a part...the hackers, the freedom fighters and so on? What about the Controllers? Are they part of the game too?"

"A better question is: if the Controllers are part of the game, who's really pulling the strings?" Frank pondered. "I know one thing: There is what we call the Shadow behind all of existence—what some still call the spiritual realm. What it is, is difficult to discern. Knowing anymore about it, well, that's simply not part of our programming."

"So you can't break out of the game?" I asked.

"To be honest with you, I don't know. I've seen no credible evidence that you can," Frank replied, reaching up and removing the pot on his head. For the first time, we could see his real head, short black hair and all. He replaced the pot with a skullcap made of tinfoil that came to a peak in the center of his skull. Poking out of the peak was a small red feather. "But the battle right now is to determine who will control the programs."

It was difficult to focus on what Frank was saying. I couldn't stop staring at his new topper.

"Had to change headgear," he explained with a shrug. "The pot gets heavy."

"And the feather?" I asked.

"Oh, that's just to avoid looking so dreary," he said with a bashful grin.

Eileen laughed out loud, flashing a sparkling glance at me.

Gordon cleared his throat, a clear sign that we needed to get back to business.

"Yes, yes. Time is a'wasting, Gordon," Frank conceded. "The task at hand: we believe that if we can infiltrate the Hive, we can disrupt their central energy site. That's how they thrive—off our energy. That's how they maintain their system of oppression and control. But if we can disrupt their energy systems, then we can lessen their control over us."

"And that's where we come in, right?" Eileen asked.

"Exactly," Frank nodded. "Now the only way we're going to be able to get you into the Hive undetected is to make you invisible to the naked eye."

"You can do that?" I asked.

"It's still in the experimental phase, but yes, we can create the impression of invisibility through a process called re-digitalization," Frank said. "We'll start with a demonstration. As you will see, there will appear to be nothing to the visible eye until Gordon here employs this handheld scanner."

"But how does it work?" Eileen asked.

"When you are re-digitalized, your body's molecular structure is broken down and reassembled in another form—one not visible to the naked eye," Frank explained. "It creates the illusion of invisibility, like a ghost."

Pausing, he glanced over at Gordon.

"Slide the molecular destabilizer over here," Frank directed Gordon. "Time to give it a whirl."

Gordon slid a tall, two-sided machine toward Frank's desk, leaving it parked just to the right of the desk.

"Ready when you are, Frank," came the reply.

"It's what has been called remote viewing in that you can penetrate time and space and move unimpeded through material objects," Microwave Man continued. "One important cautionary note: when you are destabilized and invisible, avoid, at all costs, passing through so-called normal human beings."

"Why?" I asked.

"There is a tendency to accumulate the nature of the living objects that you pass through," Frank said, pointing his finger at us. "You certainly don't want to pick up any evil tendencies of those you'll be visiting topside."

Microwave Man moved between the two wire-infused towers and removed his tinfoil bonnet. "Okay, turn on the juice, Gordon. Once I've re-digitalized, scan me and show our students what it means to really go undercover."

"Will do," Gordon said. He flipped a small red lever on the front side of one of the twin towers. "Brrrr, brrr, brrr, brrr!" the machine screeched, followed by what sounded like something short-circuiting.

I watched Frank slowly fade into thin air.

Talk about a mind-blowing experience.

Eileen looked equally dumbfounded. "I'd heard rumors about this, but it's incredible."

"Let's give it a few," Gordon murmured, glancing over at us. "I'll scan the room for our disappearing mad scientist."

Finally, Gordon stepped up behind Frank's desk and held his scanning device in front of him, moving it from side to side. "There. Turn and take a look."

As I cautiously looked over my shoulder, I could see the outline of a human figure walking behind us. It was glittering and quivering as if it would blow up at any second.

"Show 'em how you can penetrate so-called material objects, Frank," Gordon directed.

Moving rather quickly around us and facing his desk, Microwave Man walked through it as if the desk were not there—as if the desk, too, were an illusion.

"How about waving to our mind-boggled students?" Gordon asked. The electronic creature in front of us began waving frantically.

"Do you guys get the picture?" Gordon asked.

"Without a doubt," Eileen said, still staring at the oscillating vision before us in amazement.

"Alright," Gordon said as Frank reentered the destabilizer. Gordon again flipped the red switch. And with the same whirring sound, Frank slowly materialized before our astonished eyes.

"Alakazam with a bit of strawberry jam!" Stepping out from between the twin towers, Microwave Man walked to the front of his desk. "Well, what do you think?"

"Unbelievable," I said.

"The big question," Eileen asked, scrutinizing Frank carefully. "Does that do any harm to your body?"

"Not that I've experienced, as long as you avoid passing through other living beings," Frank replied.

"Is that all it can do?" I asked.

"Isn't that enough?" Gordon asked.

"There is the possibility of time travel if we can master how to change our brains' receiving abilities," Frank said, very serious now. "The material world is merely one of many parallel universes. You, my friend, are trapped in this one as long as you believe it."

"The only world we need to worry about right now is this one, however," Gordon interrupted testily. "Time is of the essence."

"Gordon is right," Frank said. "Which one of you would like to experience re-digitalization first?"

"Let me be your guinea pig," I volunteered.

"Fine with me," Frank said. "Step up beside the destabilization unit."

Rising from my chair, I walked around Frank's desk and faced the whirring machine. "A word of caution: your body will feel an electric tingling sensation as you destabilize," Microwave Man said.

"Thanks for the warning."

"Also," Frank warned. "Once you've gone over to the other side, we can track you. Be sure, and let me emphasize, be sure to follow my instructions. Are you listening?"

"That I am," I replied.

"Okay, step into the machine. Gordon will flip the lever."

I stepped between the two electronic towers. Gordon reached down and flipped the lever. A humming sound filled my ears. At first, I felt nothing, then the tingling sensation seeped into every fiber of my being. I tried to speak, but my lips were frozen together. I reached up to loosen my lips and my hand went through my skull. I was now re-digitalized.

"Okay, Erik. Step forward. We are tracking you. Wave your right hand if you can hear me." I did as Frank directed. "Alright. See if you can walk through my desk and stop in front of Eileen."

Again, I did as directed. I walked through the desk as if it wasn't there.

"I can see you, Erik. How are you doing?" Eileen asked.

I started to wave my hand when I caught sight of a strange figure stepping towards me. It was Orwell, the man with the manuscript who died in front of me, on the pavement. Before I could signal or call out to him, he vanished as quickly as he had appeared.

"Okey-dokey, Erik. Circle around and reenter the machine and we'll bring you back," Frank said.

Standing inside the machine, I felt the tingling sensation again. My body returned to its former state. "You won't believe what happened," I said, stepping out from between the towers. "I saw the guy... the dead guy from the pavement..."

"Not possible, kid," Frank said. "But we can debate it later. Let's have Eileen take a turn first."

Eileen shot me a quick look, rose, entered the machine, and disappeared. Frank conducted the same drill with her and then brought her home again.

"Now, that's an experience!" she said, sitting down beside me.

"We're at the next step now. First..." Frank stopped abruptly, his eyes rolling back in his head.

"The Controllers are on the hunt," Frank screamed. "They're moving to destroy. They've got him. He's theirs now. Smash! Kill! He's leading a Werewolf Unit!"

"Grab his head shield!" Gordon instructed, holding Frank down. "He's getting bombarded. Hurry!"

I leapt forward, grabbed the tin foil hat from Frank's desk, and quickly stuck it on his head.

"Gordon, is he okay?" Eileen asked.

"Yeah. Give him a few seconds," Gordon said, peering at Frank intensely.

"It was him," Microwave Man said, reaching for Eileen. "They've turned him."

"It was Lucian, wasn't it?" Eileen asked.

With a slight pause, Frank nodded.

Eileen nodded, her chin trembling.

"We'll get him back, if there's a way," I murmured, rubbing her arm.

"The quicker you get started, the better," Gordon said, staring into Frank's glazed pupils.

"We need to put them through the destabilizing units a few more times," Microwave Man said.

"Let's get it done," Gordon said, running Eileen and me through the destabilizing drill several times before Frank was satisfied.

"Tomorrow, you'll begin your journey to the dark side," Frank said after we'd run through the last drill. "You'll pass through various places in the Outer World before you reach your destination. You will return home for a little while before taking a shot at the target."

"Thanks for the briefing," Eileen said, reaching out and hugging Microwave Man.

"Okay, Gordon, escort our friends to safety. Spidus will be calling on them soon for final instructions."

"Be on high alert," Frank warned as a parting shot. "No one is safe. They want to destroy us all."

CHAPTER 21
BEFORE THE HAMMER FALLS

"Our plan is for you to collect surveillance. And if it's possible, disrupt the system. It may be our only chance before the hammer falls."—Spidus

The next morning, Johnny Dolphin showed up to escort us to a meeting with Spidus. Thin and gaunt, he had skin so white it looked like new-fallen snow. And he had a strange shuffling walk that seemed to be half a skip and half a slither.

"Spidus would like to see you. He's waiting," Dolphin squeaked.

"We'll be there in a moment," Eileen called out to Dolphin's already retreating form. He waved a hand in acknowledgment and stood at a distance, waiting.

At my questioning glance, Eileen whispered, "Johnny was born with a fin down his back. A mutation brought about by some of the drugs the populace are forced to ingest. The fin had to be surgically removed, leaving him with a deformed spine."

Dolphin escorted us to Spidus' door, then shuffled back to his duties.

Ginger was standing at silent attention on one side of Spidus' bed, his usual smirk on his face.

"How are you feeling?" Eileen asked.

"I'm getting weaker," Spidus rasped. "More trouble breathing than I'm used to. No time to waste."

Spidus nodded at Ginger.

"Eyes on the screen," Ginger instructed. "I'm going to lay out a plan of action for you two. As we speak, it's being encrypted onto Eileen's brain chip."

On the screen, a map flickered into clarity, a trail through my old world. Marked with a strange red effervescent color, it wound through various streets, many of which I had traversed.

"Why does that path lead to Academy Five?" I asked.

Ginger snorted. "That hallowed institution of learning is the entrance to the Hive."

"You mean—?" I gulped.

"Yes," Ginger sneered. "That is where the Queen runs the show. And this," he motioned to an overhead screen which revealed a set of double doors leading to the engineering room of my school, "is the point of entry for the Hive."

"We'll be able to pass through the wall, right?" Eileen asked.

"If all goes as planned, yes," Ginger said. "You'll be re-digitalized. So entrance will be easy. I hope."

"The priority is for you to collect surveillance," Spidus wheezed, turning his head toward us. "If it's possible, disrupt the system. It may be our only chance before the hammer falls."

"This should help," Ginger said, pointing to a small cylinder. "It will allow you to materialize long enough to do damage, but it only contains enough power to strike once."

"Once you use this stabilizer, run," Spidus warned, his voice whisper-soft. "Time will be short."

"We'll make haste," Eileen promised, glancing at me.

"Each of you will have one," Ginger added as he handed us the gadgets.

"It's possible that if they do a microwave sweep of their headquarters, they will be able to detect your presence, even though you'll be naked to the visible eye." Spidus strained to make himself heard. "Still, that's a chance we'll have to take."

I nodded while two words played over and over in my head: suicide mission, suicide mission, suicide …

"Ginger, get them to Frank for destabilization," Spidus ordered, his weakened voice still as authoritative as ever.

Leaning down, Eileen kissed Spidus gently on the cheek. We followed Ginger to Microwave Man's work lab.

Frank looked up as we entered.

"The mission is a go!" Ginger declared, nodding once to Eileen, directing his usual sneer my way, and then wheeling around and slamming the door behind him.

"Have a seat," Frank said. "You've been through the drill. Are you ready for the real thing?"

"As ready as I'll ever be," I said with a shrug.

Eileen reached over and grabbed my hand. "We can do this," she said, her chin jutting out with resolve.

"Right, we CAN do this," I agreed, squeezing her hand. "Team Lucian it is." At my words, her eyes misted over and she leaned in as if she had something more to say.

Frank chose that moment to clear his throat. Loudly.

"Again, just a word of caution. Avoid, if you can, passing through other human beings while you are destabilized," Frank said, giving us a nervous look. "It could disrupt the flow of molecules, making you visible to the enemy. And you certainly do not want to pick up any of their molecular defects."

"Right," I murmured, glancing at Eileen, whose hand still rested on mine. "Avoid contact with the enemy."

"Step up, Eileen," Frank instructed, pointing at the destabilizer sitting next to his desk. "I'll destabilize you first. Once you're clear, be sure to step away from the destabilizer to make room for Erik. While you will be visible to one another, you will be invisible to the rest of the world."

Eileen positioned herself between the twin towers and looked at me with a smile.

"Bzzzt, bzzzt, bzzzt," the machine blurted as Frank flipped the switch. Eileen slowly vanished.

I was up next. I positioned myself where Eileen had been seen just moments before.

Frank's finger pressed against the button.

A buzzing sound hit my eardrums.

As my body dissolved into thin air, the vague outline of Eileen's body came into view.

"Okay, you two. There's a lot riding on you, so be careful. Float away and up topside. We'll be tracking your movements from here on out. For freedom," Frank said with a brief salute.

I looked at Eileen. "For freedom and for Lucian," I pledged.

My feet slowly lifted off the ground. My body hit the ceiling and passed through it. I was disembodied and disoriented. For a moment, I could feel a surge of panic welling up in me as I prepared to chart a course through a hidden world where evil lurked.

Then Eileen grabbed hold of my hand.

The panic subsided.

I wasn't alone.

CHAPTER 22
THE PANDORA COMPLEX

"Nothing here but circus freaks, boys. We're looking for a different kind of freak show. Troublemakers. Extremists. Nonconformists. When we find them—and we will find them—we'll make them scream."—Lucian

We emerged into the noisy, topside world of teeming streets and bright flashing billboards. Large screens attached to tall buildings beamed out smiling faces, pitching various products: shoes, clothes, screen devices, toys and the like. It was a glittering land of commercialization.

The hazy, brown air enveloped us. People were yelling and screaming. About a block ahead of us, an Atlas Four cut through a crowded sidewalk. People darted in every direction to avoid falling prey to the robotic menace.

Just then, a young kid—no more than 12 or 13—raced across the street with two roboflies buzzing behind him in hot pursuit. No one stopped to help him.

"One more lesson from the world topside," I muttered under my breath. "Step out of line and get stung."

"Erik, that's our street up ahead," Eileen said.

"We need to take a right at the corner," I said. "That will take us straight to Academy Five."

The Academy towers loomed in the distance.

"How'd you wind up in Subterranea?" I asked as we began our trek towards the campus.

"I was snatched—literally—and pulled down into the wormhole before I could be hauled off to a camp for a-socials," Eileen explained. "I was preparing to enter Academy Five and had been working as the editor of our e-newsletter at my prep school. I challenged one of my professors about statements he was making about some police shootings. That's all it took for me to be brought before the school administrator and threatened with re-education. Lucian was already working with Spidus, although I didn't know it at the time. Spidus and his crew got to me before the re-programmers did."

"Let's see if we can't return the favor and snatch Lucian back," I said as we paused in front of Academy Five's stately entrance.

Eileen smiled faintly.

We passed through the unopened doors without any blips. Students walked here and there on their way to somewhere or nowhere. The information desk with its many chairs was filled with the usual heavily armed guards, dressed in their dark black military outfits and gear.

"We enter by way of the engineering complex on Level X," I whispered. "Let's take the elevator."

"No need to whisper," Eileen replied in a normal tone. "We're occupying a different dimension right now, so they can't see or hear us."

We hovered behind a bald guy dressed in a gray suit who was waiting for the elevator. "Only classified personnel can enter the elevator, but I suppose we can break a few rules," I said with a smile.

"X is the lowest level, where the scientists and engineers work," Eileen said. "They go around in full, sealed body units so that they are completely encased."

As the doors opened, the man in gray stepped squarely in front of a facial recognition device. "Screened!" the disembodied voice of the scanning device announced. "You are approved to enter."

On either side of the doors, swiveling laser blasters were mounted to ward off any suspected trespassers.

Tight security.

This was the first test…to see if we could pass through the screening undetected. Holding our breaths, we entered the elevator. No alarm sounded. First hurdle down.

The doors quickly closed and we began to descend. Standing on either side of our fellow traveler, I chanced a look at him. He had the look of a rodent. Round eyeglasses rested on a very pointed nose. His two front teeth peeked through his lips.

After a slow descent, the doors opened and the elevator's robotic voice announced, "Level X. Please exit. 10 seconds until liftoff. Nine. Eight…"

We followed the needle-nosed man as he rushed out of the elevator and hurried away.

Spread out before us was a sea of turbines and generators whirring as they stored energy and dispensed it to the world above. Eileen nudged me to proceed straight ahead.

Workers were moving here and there, most of them in quickstep.

To my left, one of the workers—head covered with a baseball hat, face swathed in gauze and strange luminous eyes peering out through dark goggles—looked our way.

"Do you think Gauzeman senses us?" I asked Eileen.

She glanced over at him. "Perhaps, but he can't see us or he'd be sending up an alarm. That gauze is actually a protective wrap to shield him from the high radiation down here. This place is run by a nuclear reactor and it ain't friendly to humans."

A robotic animal of some kind passed in front of us. Like a large bear, it had metallic teeth and green gleaming eyes. Suddenly, without warning, it started galloping in the direction of one of the workers, who gave a yell and began to flee. The android monster took a long leap and landed on its prey, dragging the worker to the ground.

A voice screamed, "Please no! No! Please no!" It was a young girl being mauled by the metal fangs.

I looked over at Eileen.

"We can't risk it," she replied, her eyes filling with tears. "We're destabilized and we've got to stay that way. At least until our mission is complete."

The girl's screams grew shrill, then hoarse, then choked out by the blood gurgling in her throat. As she lay limp, the robotic bear stalked off, looking to the left and right. A cleanup crew waited to approach the body until the bear was out of sight.

Eileen gestured for me to follow her.

We continued walking. The path before us narrowed and darkened until we were face to face with a large, circular steel net. It barricaded the entrance to a lit, glowing tunnel.

We stopped at the tunnel entrance. Eileen turned to me. "This doorway leads to the Pandora Complex. This is their central energizing center."

"This is how they maintain control?" I asked.

"More than that," Eileen replied. "It's the main source of their life force. We're going to pass through this grating. We'll enter here and de-elevate several stories down to another level that exists below here."

"And we won't be detected?"

"This is a high radiation point," she said. "They would not expect any uninvited visitors entering here. It's sure death to human cells. But we are destabilized."

Moving side by side, we dissolved through the grate and entered the luminous tunnel. We walked several hundred feet until Eileen stopped. "We can drop here. This will put us just inside the complex," she said, reaching for my hand.

"Let's go," I said. We dropped rapidly but with a floating sensation. I felt like an astronaut descending onto some forbidden planet. Flashes of light and strange shadows—shadows with human forms—flew by.

As my feet hit solid matter, a strange sparkling metallic curtain appeared in front of us.

"We've got to pass through it," Eileen whispered, giving my hand a reassuring squeeze.

I took the lead and melted through the folding metallic curtain only to stop short on the other side, recoiling in horror. I heard Eileen's gasp of dismay, but I couldn't look away from what was before us.

Life-sized test tubes occupied the room. They contained half human, half machine-like creatures floating in a glowing, yellowish, amniotic fluid the color of urine.

Some of the test-tube creatures had human appendages. Some were armed with mechanical, robot-like claws. Some had wheels where legs should be but were human otherwise: arms, hands and all.

Some had human bodies but the heads of animals—pigs, hawks, alligators, and goats. One had what seemed to be a velociraptor head. Others were small-bodied creatures with large extraterrestrial heads.

Eileen leaned forward, her head mere inches from a glass tube, to study a raptor-headed human. It slowly opened its large reptilian eyes and stared back. Eileen jumped back and grabbed my arm.

"It can see us, can't it?" I asked. "Somehow, it knows we're here."

Eileen said nothing, caught up in the raptor's stare.

"Eileen, what are these things?" I asked.

She finally looked away from the raptor. "These are experimental successes. Remember the morgue at the Violence Reduction Center? We saw similar creatures, but they were dead experiments gone wrong."

From the corner of my eyes, I sensed movement. I turned just in time to pull Eileen aside and avoid being cell-merged with a group of technicians and scientists in white coats who had entered behind us.

They patrolled the space with screen devices, walking, stopping, taking notes and occasionally talking to one another. Some moved in between and around the test-tube creatures.

I signaled to Eileen and started edging around the group of white coats only to stop short again. Standing a short distance from the rest of the group was a man dressed in the same white outfit, but he was a hybrid creature of sorts—with two small horns and large deer-like legs, hooves and all.

"Pan, are you keeping up with our newest unit?" an old, horn-rimmed technician asked the goatman.

"Yes, sir," Pan replied. "We're having some trouble, but I do believe we can sustain it. Hopefully, it will live."

The technician pointed towards one of the tubes as Pan followed. Several others trailed behind him.

Suddenly, a slow, barking noise broke the whirring silence of the room. Four scowling men—dressed in the dark uniforms of cops—with a bevy of weapons attached to their waists stormed into the room, slamming the metal doors behind them. Eileen and I edged further away to avoid them coming into contact with our destabilized bodies.

Glancing at the lead guy, I froze.

It was Lucian.

I stepped forward, intending to do what, exactly, I couldn't say.

Eileen grabbed my arm and pulled me back. "Not yet," she cautioned. "He looks like Lucian, but he may not be *our* Lucian anymore. We need to wait and see."

We didn't have long to wait.

This Lucian was clearly in charge. Stepping forward, he surveyed the room with a penetrating stare.

Briefly, his gaze lingered where Eileen and I had squeezed ourselves into a corner. Something flashed in his eyes and then it was gone. He turned away and focused on the assembled, white-coated workers.

"We received an alert from one of our contacts in the underground," Lucian announced in a terse, cold tone that was completely unlike the Lucian I knew. "We may have some visitors trying to infiltrate the complex."

One of the technicians looked around and shrugged his shoulder. "Same old cast of characters here."

Lucian glared, growled and twitched, then swaggered forward, weaving his way among the technicians and scientists, all of whom scurried to clear a path for him.

Every few feet, he stopped to peer at a particular worker or demand identification, or gaze at one of the creatures floating in the tubes.

Everything about him screamed "menace."

Pausing in front of the tube with the raptor-headed human, Lucian reached out and tapped on the glass. The creature blinked open its eyes and stared back at Lucian.

Before Lucian could do anything more, Pan stepped in front of him, blocking his access to the tube. "These are sensitive experiments," he bleated. "You cannot be in here without first going through decontamination!"

"Rude pig," Lucian growled, stepping back. "I can be wherever I please." With one last glance at the raptor hybrid, whose gaze had now shifted over to where Eileen and I stood, invisible and silent in the corner, Lucian turned with military precision and finished his scrutiny of the room's occupants.

"Nothing here but circus freaks, boys," Lucian finally concluded, signaling to his black-clad storm troopers to head out. "We're looking for a different kind of freak show. Troublemakers. Extremists. Nonconformists. When we find them—and we will find them—we'll make them scream."

With a final glance that lingered briefly over the empty corner where we stood, Lucian—or what used to be the man we knew as Lucian—exited the room.

CHAPTER 23
A FRACTURED FAIRYTALE

"Ghello loved her father, King Rhion, but her desire for power became so all-consuming that she traded her heart for her father's throne."—Eileen

There was no time to process what we had seen or wonder at how quickly the Controllers had managed to transform Lucian the Resister into Lucian the Tormentor.

Moments after Lucian and his goons exited the complex, a tall man entered, shrouded in a dark garment with a hood that covered most of his head except for his face, which was dominated by eyes the size of golf balls. He waved his arms at the technicians, directing them to gather around him. Pan joined the group with a goat-like skip, buck and a leap.

"Quickly," Eileen said, signaling for me to follow as we approached the gathering.

"The Queen commands our presence," shouted the hooded man, his voice sounding like a robot, very precise and edgy. "Follow me," he instructed Pan and two white-clothed technicians, who immediately trailed behind.

"Let's go," Eileen said. "This may be our best chance to get close to the Queen of the Hive."

We hurriedly followed the group, which was almost jogging now. As we stepped past some sliding doors, we entered a wide hallway where two black-clad, heavily armed guards were waiting. "We have orders from the Queen. She commands our presence," the bug-eyed one proclaimed.

"Yes," one of the armed guards said, his right eye covered over with a black patch. "You know the protocol, Morris," the guard said. "Be sure to go over the routine with your people. No surprises."

Morris shrugged and turned to the small group. "If you want to survive your audience with Her Highness without being maimed or killed, walk slowly and enunciate your words and speak slowly but only when and if you are asked a question," Morris advised. "Otherwise, keep the lips zipped. She gets irritated very easily. Also, show no emotion. Keep your eyes on her just in case she looks your way. Understood?"

The technicians nodded their heads in unison.

"Understood," Pan replied.

"Now that that's out of the way, you can follow me," the cop who looked like a pirate said. "We will be descending quite a distance. I've cleared your entry."

At that, the cop turned with Morris and the technicians in tow and headed down the hallway.

Approaching some more elevator doors with armed guards positioned on both sides, the group waited for the doors to open. Eileen and I quickly followed behind the entourage as they entered the elevator. The doors closed swiftly.

Turning and facing the doors, with the technicians behind him, the cop, looking over his shoulder, proclaimed, "Hail to the Queen!"

All in the elevator repeated the mantra in unison.

No one spoke a word again until the doors opened and the cop ordered, "Everyone out! Wait in the Blue Room. Your systems will be analyzed to ensure security for Her Majesty."

The group exited the elevator and strode down an ornamented hallway littered with old paintings. Garlands and wallpaper adorned the walls. Victorian-era type stuff. It was like stepping back in time except for the scanners and surveillance devices that kept constant watch.

"Here's the Blue Room," the cop announced, opening a door. "You'll be summoned soon."

"Fine," Morris said.

Eileen nudged me and pointed to a distant corner. "Head over there," she whispered. "While we wait, I can fill you in on the Queen."

"Have you seen the Queen before?" I asked.

Eileen shook her head. "I haven't, but Spidus has. I don't know the exact circumstances, but he filled me in on the parts of her history he's been able to piece together."

"So how'd she get to be Queen?" I asked.

"Before she was the Queen of the Hive, she was Ghello. Her parents ruled as the king and queen of Mars."

"You mean Mars, the red planet, the fourth planet from the sun?"

"That's the one. In their day, Mars was a peaceful, lush, beautiful planet."

"From what I know, there's nothing peaceful, lush or beautiful about Mars," I pointed out.

"This is before it was destroyed by warring factions," Eileen said. "I'll get to that part in a moment."

I glanced over to where the lab workers were being run through security scans and threat detections. "You might want to speed this fairytale up."

"Ghello was surrounded by courtiers and advisers who had devised a plot to take over the kingdom," Eileen said as she leaned back against the wall. "They persuaded her that she was so special—the greatest among all on Mars and even in history—that she deserved to rule."

"So what did she do? Knock off her old lady and old man?"

"Not quite. Ghello loved her father, King Rhion, but her desire for power became so all-consuming that she traded her heart for her father's throne." Eileen shrugged. "She allowed Malkin, her chief advisor and confidant, to drain all the love, kindness and empathy out of her, and store it in a device that Malkin keeps in his possession."

"That's some fractured fairytale," I said.

"Yes," Eileen agreed, "and from that day on, Ghello became the monster she is. She had her mother and father imprisoned in a dungeon where they died."

"So how'd she get here?"

"Ghello is greedy but not wise." Eileen chewed on her bottom lip. "Under her rule, Mars was torn apart by endless, monstrous wars, until there was nothing left to fight over. So she fled here and became the reigning demon. Now she rules over the Hive here on this planet."

"So how long ago was this?"

"According to Spidus, Ghello came here centuries ago," Eileen replied. "All those ancient monuments ... the pyramids, Stonehenge and so on? Early civilizations didn't have the technology to build them, but Ghello did. She hid behind the scenes manipulating all the killings and blood rituals, the sacrificing of children and virgins that occurred at various places throughout the ancient world."

"I get the killings, but what's with the blood?" I asked.

"The Queen subsists on human blood and maintains her life force by consuming it," Eileen explained.

"Sounds more like a vampire story than a fairytale," I said. "It's a shame we can't just expose her to sunlight and let her meet her doom that way."

Before Eileen could respond, a new set of guards entered the room. "All gather," they announced. "You have been commanded to enter and await the Queen's arrival!"

CHAPTER 24
PEACE THROUGH
TYRANNY

"Move forward with the new order so that we might unite the upper, middle and lower realms. The time has come for my rule to be all-encompassing."—Ghello, Queen of the Hive

The group, which had swelled to three dozen people, had been directed down yet another hallway and was waiting outside yet another set of double doors.

Two guards with black-as-coal, Lucian-type eyes stood at attention on either side of the doors.

With a swoosh, the doors opened and a voice loudly commanded, "Step forward one by one. You'll be scanned once again for clearance."

"We don't want to go through this scanner and risk detection," Eileen said, grabbing my hand and leading me around the group being scanned and through the wall to the right of the double doors.

Having bypassed the scanners, we watched as the guests filtered through the final security checkpoint into a smaller anteroom of sorts. Devoid of any furniture or décor, its only distinguishing feature was a large, black, ornamental door with large, silver handles.

"Wait here for Malkin," a heavily armed guard said, signaling for the entourage to stand to one side.

"The Queen's throne room is probably located behind those," Eileen said, pointing to the door, which had just opened to allow a tall, dark male figure to pass through.

"That's Malkin, the Queen's right-hand man," Eileen whispered as the man approached the group. He had black hair that extended all the way down his back and walked with a silent, panther-like gait, a long, silver staff in his hand.

I nudged Eileen. "Take a look at the baton he's holding," I murmured. The silver staff had been molded to resemble a slender, twisted tree branch covered in strange runes. Embedded into the top of the staff, protected by a cross-hatching of smaller branches that formed a cage, was a gleaming red orb that pulsed with an inner light.

"Could it be—?" Eileen asked.

"—the Queen's heart? You said Malkin keeps it with him always."

"So it's true," Eileen said. "Spidus will want to hear about this."

Malkin had yet to address the group, but indicated with a slight nod of the head for them to follow him. He led them through the massive black door into a cavernous, circular room lined with red velvet drapes.

A massive throne made out of glass—it appeared to be an elaborate fish tank filled with shifting, swirling colors—dominated the front of the room. Over the throne, a backlit, glittering, stained-glass window—its panels made up of deep, jewel tones—bathed the throne in a wash of light. A long, red carpet bisected the throne room, lining the walkway from the doorway to the throne.

Again, Malkin wordlessly directed the group to assemble on either side of the red carpet. He then turned and made his way on the red carpet toward the throne, where he stood at attention.

"I want to take a closer look at that throne," I said to Eileen. "Wait here."

"Look, but don't linger," Eileen warned. "Whatever you do, don't stare directly into the throne."

I didn't understand what Eileen meant about not staring into the throne until I got close to it.

What I had assumed to be a tank filled with colorful fish was in fact a large glass tomb in the shape of a throne filled with writhing human bodies in a sea of glowing orange amniotic fluid.

The faces of naked men, women, children—even babies—lined the inner walls of the throne. They were packed together tightly, so that only their faces could be seen peering out, while their bodies had been contorted and twisted around each other within the inner regions of the tank. Their bright red eyes were open and stared unblinkingly at the room's occupants.

My attention was caught by a small child, a girl with her hair swirling in the amniotic fluid. Almost too late, I remembered Eileen's warning and looked away just as the child's gaze shifted towards where I stood, invisible. For a moment, it seemed as if she was attempting to talk to me, but no sound came from her lips.

I hurried back to Eileen and reported what I had seen.

"It makes sense, in a twisted way," she said, her eyes drawn to the throne. "It's difficult to escape the parent connection. Rhion ruled from what he called the Seat of the Eye, an all-seeing throne of eyes or surveillance devices that helped him keep order. It sounds like Ghello has created her own Throne of Eyes."

"I don't know if they're actually alive or if their bodies are merely conduits, but their eyes do seem to be alert and monitoring the room," I said.

Eileen chewed on her thumb reflexively. "Rhion used surveillance devices as his eyes. Perhaps Ghello has wired these human eyes to act as surveillance devices and feed her data."

"If that's part of her Hive, I can only imagine what this Queen looks like," I said with a shudder.

"Ghello's goal is to create a hybrid race of beings—half demon and half human—with supernatural powers," Eileen said quietly.

"More like a race of monsters," I said, thinking of the creatures we had seen in the complex earlier.

"Wom, wom, wom, wom!" A whirring electronic siren blared through the room. All eyes turned toward Malkin, who had stepped in front of the throne. "The Queen will be in our presence shortly. Prepare yourselves."

A shrill scream penetrated the air around us. Overhead, the ceiling slowly began to open as a sparkling, dazzling lightshow lit the room.

From the opening in the ceiling emerged feet covered in hawk-like bird shoes, long talons and all. Long, slender legs encased in leather and framed by a gauzy skirt were followed by a trim, fit midsection and an upper body with a regal bearing.

Ghello was floating down from the ceiling like a demonic angel.

Her hands had long thin fingers that resembled iron-like sickles. She landed in front of the throne, large leather wings protruding from either side of her back. Still, it was her head that blew my mind. A beautiful face covered in a greenish-blue skin and furious, bloodshot orbs. What at first glance looked like a strange psychedelic hairdo turned out to be writhing, wriggling serpents.

"What the—" I said, looking at Eileen.

"According to our intel, the snake beings on her head are robotic cameras, sensors and other surveillance devices that feed an incredible amount of information into her mind," Eileen explained.

"Glad to be among you again," Ghello proclaimed in a sweet, melodious voice. "I welcome you."

The Queen's tongue—long, red and serpentine—shot forth from her mouth for a second, hung in the air and retreated to hide behind her full, red lips.

The gathering bowed their heads in unison, worshipfully.

"I am ready for your report, Dr. Mengele," the Queen said, the swirling serpents on her head twisting to focus on each and every individual present. "I do hope all is in order for the hybrid army?"

Stepping forward into the center aisle, a short man in a black suit, white shirt and black tie affirmed. "Yes, Your Majesty," Mengele said, bowing his head. "We have succeeded in stage two of the creation and stabilization of the hybrids."

The gathering broke forth into applause as the Queen nodded approvingly.

"Move forward with the new order so that we might unite the upper, middle and lower realms," the Queen ordered. "The time has come for my rule to be all-encompassing."

"What is she talking about?" I asked Eileen.

"It sounds like she wants to use her hybrid army to bring the world topside and those beneath the earth under her control," Eileen explained.

"There will be resistance, but it will be easily vanquished," the Queen said with a beaming smile that exposed enormous, silvery teeth that sparkled in the light. "Do you agree, Mengele?"

"Yes. Quite," Mengele nodded. "We are but a few months away from completing our work on the hybrids. Once complete, our army will be trained and prepared to serve at your command, Majesty."

"The possibilities for this new world are endless," the Queen declared, as her multi-headed device began writhing again. Mengele nodded once again in agreement, then turned to face the group to see if anyone dared speak.

"Peace through tyranny is our mantra," the Queen proclaimed. "Let me hear you!"

"Peace through tyranny! Peace through tyranny!" the assembled crowd chanted.

"If anyone dare step in our path, then annihilation is ..." the Queen boomed out. She stopped midsentence, her piercing eyes surveying the crowd, the tentacles on her head flipping about in a frenzy. "I sense a strange presence in the room. Malkin, did you and the guards properly vet everyone before they entered my chambers?"

"Yes, your Majesty!" Malkin confirmed.

"Someone in this chamber is not one of us," the Queen murmured, her wings flapping slowly behind her. "No, not some *one* ... there are two traitors among us."

"Death to tyrants!" came a loud, piercing bleat.

Pan, the goat-headed technician, leapt into the center aisle and ran headlong at the Queen, his horns aimed straight at her.

The Queen needed no guards to jump to her defense. Before he could get close enough to do any damage, the Queen's serpentine tongue— inhumanly long and engorged—shot forth from her mouth, wrapped itself around Pan's neck, and proceeded to strangle him.

Pan's eyes bulged. His face turned red. With one last, choking gasp, he muttered, "Death to tyrants."

The Queen's tongue uncoiled from around the dead body. Pan's lifeless corpse dropped to the ground. "Death to the Resistance is more apropos," the Queen sneered, kicking at Pan's body. "Anyone for some goats' head soup?"

The entourage twittered nervously.

"Silence!" The Queen again peered into the crowd. "I still feel the presence of two entities."

"Perhaps you are sensing the remnants of the goat's life force, Your Majesty?" Mengele suggested. "Your sensors might be picking up on his hybridization and interpreting them as two entities."

The Queen tilted her head in consideration as she began to weave a path through the assembled workers.

"It's us," Eileen said, grabbing my arm and pulling me away from the group. "Her devices are reading our electromagnetic waves. Melt through the back doors. Run, Erik! Run!"

As we turned, ran and passed through the doors and hurtled down the hallway, the Queen issued a bloodcurdling cry. "Who dares to breach my inner sanctum?" she screamed. "Reveal yourself!"

"Let's go straight up through the ceiling," Eileen said. She grabbed me by the hand, and we began to ascend. We passed through layer after layer of steel, earth and bone—both human and animal—striated throughout the earth's strata.

I grew lightheaded from ascending so quickly. Finally, we reached the surface.

We emerged onto a busy thoroughfare. Cars and buses careened through our destabilized bodies. "Head for the sidewalk," Eileen said.

I didn't feel right. My skin began to tingle. My ears felt like caverns. I was gasping for air. I could smell the pale brown air as it rolled up on my face and into my nostrils.

"Something's wrong," I choked out.

"We're starting to stabilize," Eileen said. "Something has definitely gone wrong. We're coming back too soon."

CHAPTER 25
THE QUEEN'S TOOL

"I am no one's tool, sister dear."—Lucian

"We can't materialize out here," I said, struggling to keep it together. "We'll be like sitting ducks."

"We've got to blend in," Eileen said, dodging a cyclist. "You know the drill. You've lived it your whole life."

"Where are we headed?"

"We've got to get back to the antique shop. It's the closest access point," she replied.

"That's still a ways off." Before I could suggest we find somewhere to take cover, Eileen screamed, "Run, Erik, run!" as she was lifted up and away from me.

The Atlas Fours had us surrounded.

There was no time to react. I was the next to be grabbed and pulled up by one of the gigantic claws.

Now Eileen and I were side-by-side and in the clutches of two tectronic monsters.

"You are under arrest for terrorist activities," one of our robotic captors announced. "We will now proceed to central headquarters for interrogation."

"Put me down you metal ape," Eileen yelled.

"Silence, civilian, or you will be silenced," ordered the metallic fiend.

I attempted to kick out my captor's sensor shield, but it was no use.

"This behavior will not be tolerated," declared the Atlas Four.

Just then, a stinging sensation ripped through my body. Suddenly, I was floating in a black cocoon, unconscious of time or place or self.

How long I was suspended in that black limbo I couldn't say, but at one point, I became aware of a bright, white light that grew lighter and brighter as I accelerated towards it.

I was being pulled up into a shining vortex.

The shadows around me evaporated into disconcerting, humming, flashing lights.

"Welcome, Erik," a disembodied voice murmured. "It's good to have you with us."

The faint outline of a head came into focus. "Where am I? Who are you?" I mumbled.

"Just give the juice a moment or two to fade out of your system," the soft voice said. "Then we will begin the next step on your recovery process."

"Recovery?" I was feeling a bit more clearheaded now and suddenly conscious of restraints on my arms and legs.

I squinted against the light and looked more closely at the figure leaning towards me, a thin older man with a gray beard, long gray hair pulled back in a ponytail, and the eyes of a madman.

"Good," the man said, rubbing his hands together eagerly. "You're coming out of this quickly."

"Where is Eileen?" I asked, trying to get a sense of where we were and how much trouble we were in.

"Tut tut, where are my manners?" the man said, shaking his head. "Let's get introductions out of the way first, shall we? I'm Zane, your facilitator. I'll be preparing you, along with our team, to undergo your recovery process."

"*Where* is Eileen?" I repeated, fearing the worst.

"And of course, you know Lucian," Zane continued placidly, looking to a point behind me. "He's been very anxious for you to wake up."

Footsteps approached me. I tried to raise up but straps were laced over my neck, wrists, waist, knees and my feet. Lucian's face loomed over me.

"What the hell have you done?" I growled, pulling against the restraints. "Where is Eileen?"

"Struggle all you want," Lucian said, a hint of a smile playing around his mouth. "You won't be able to squirm out of this one."

"What have you done with Eileen?" I yelled. "What have they done to *you*?"

"Done?" Lucian laughed humorlessly. "I haven't done anything to HER yet. As for ME, they've made a better man of me. We'll do the same for the two of you, I promise ... at least, we'll make a man of you. Eileen may require special treatment."

"You'd better not touch a hair on her head," I warned, straining uselessly at the straps holding me down.

"Yeah, yeah, I'm quaking with fear," Lucian said, glancing away. "Zane, why don't you put him out of his misery—this one time—and let him see his little friend?"

Zane reached over and began pushing buttons on a console beside the examining table where I lay. The table swiveled up to a standing position and turned to the left.

I was now face-to-face with Eileen, who was similarly restrained on an adjoining table. She was still unconscious. As I watched, Zane crossed over to her and injected her with something.

"Stop!" I yelled, trying to tear myself free of the manacles. "What are you doing?"

Zane glanced over at me, baring his teeth in the imitation of a smile. "Nothing to worry about ... yet," he murmured with a wicked glint in his eye. "It's just a small serum to bring her around."

The serum was fast-working.

Eileen shifted, moaned and opened her eyes. She stared at Zane blankly for a moment, then closed her eyes.

"No, no, this won't do," Lucian murmured, moving towards her. "Eileen, wake up," he ordered.

Eileen's eyes fluttered open again. Seeing Lucian, she gave a start. "Lucian? You're here? You're okay? I was so worried..." Her eyes drifted closed again.

"Bring her around," Lucian directed Zane, staring intently at Eileen. "Give her another hit of the serum if you have to."

"No!" I cried out. "Leave her alone!"

"That shouldn't be necessary," Zane said, checking Eileen's pulse point at her throat. "She just needs a wake-up call."

"I'll give her a wake-up call," Lucian said, levering Eileen's head up with one hand and slapping her sharply across the face with the other.

She cried out but slept on.

"I'll kill you for that," I swore, powerless to do anything more than rage at him. "Leave her alone! I'm the one you want."

Lucian slapped her again. This time, she woke fully, her eyes staring up at him in dismay. Her reddened cheek bore the imprint of his hand. She glanced past Lucian to me, her eyes widening in alarm at the sight of me shackled.

"Erik!" she cried out, her eyes welling up with tears. "What have they done to you?"

"Eileen, it's ok," I said. "I'm fine. We'll get out of this."

"I'm so sorry, Erik," she said, a tear spilling down her cheek. "You wouldn't be here if it weren't for me."

"I wouldn't want to be anywhere else," I pledged hoarsely.

"That was so heart-warming," Lucian drawled. "Didn't it just move you, Zane?"

Zane nodded serenely.

"Lucian, let him go!" Eileen begged. "I'm the one you want!"

"Funny, but that's exactly what Erik said," Lucian said, moving closer to me, his metallic eyes dull, dark moons. "Still, there's no time for romance in this brave new world we're forging, so let's get on with the program, shall we? We have so much to do and so little time for chit chat."

"Have you really changed so much?" I asked Lucian, trying to stall for time before whatever awaited us. "What did they do—excise your heart along with your brain?"

"What?" Lucian said, his attention clearly diverted.

"We know what they did to you," I said, glancing briefly at Eileen, hoping she would play along. "They didn't make you a better man. They turned you into a monster."

"And what is it that you think they did to me?" Lucian asked.

"They made you their tool," I replied with a deliberate smirk. "All you know how to do is salute and follow orders."

"I am no one's tool!" Lucian screamed in a high-pitched voice. In a fury, he stepped towards me, fists raised, murder in his eyes.

"Let's not get sidetracked," Zane cautioned, glancing nervously at a surveillance camera positioned over the door.

"Erik is right," Eileen said softly, halting Lucian in his tracks. "If you were still your own man and not the Queen's tool, you wouldn't need to keep us tied down like this."

"I am no one's tool, sister dear," Lucian repeated, moving towards Eileen and slapping her hard across the face. Her head slammed back against the table, but she made no sound.

He raised his hand to hit her again.

"You're not a man," I blurted out, trying desperately to draw him away from Eileen. "Real men don't need to brutalize defenseless women."

Lucian looked long and hard at Eileen, who stared back at him defiantly, then me. "Perhaps you're right," he said. "I'm not a man. I'm a wolf on the prowl, and I'm looking for worthy prey. Will that be you, do you suppose?"

"I'm a sitting duck here, so you're not going to get much of a thrill hunting me," I said, gesturing to my restraints. "If I were free to move around, however, now that might be a challenge."

"You think so?" Lucian asked. "You think you're any match for me?"

"I never had a problem beating you on the basketball court before," I said, mockingly. "I'm sure I could hold my own."

Lucian gritted his teeth, then glanced up at the surveillance camera.

"Don't do it, Lucian," Zane warned. "We've got strict orders."

"That's right, Lucian," I murmured. "You've got to follow orders, don't you?"

In a swift move, Lucian reached down, grabbed me by the neck and began to choke me. As the air was cut off from my throat, I began wheezing and gasping for air. I couldn't breathe.

"Leave him alone, you lunatic!" Eileen screamed. "You wouldn't do that if he wasn't tied up."

"But he is tied up," Lucian replied. With a satisfied grin, he released his grip on me and I started coughing. "That makes it more fun."

"I don't give a damn if you beat me, shoot me, kick me or whatever," I said, trying to get my breath. "Just let Eileen go."

"Interesting proposition, but no dice," Lucian said. "Double the trouble, double the fun. Besides, Zane has really been looking forward to our little session with you two."

"You could have twice as much fun for the price of one," I said, looking first at Zane and then at Lucian. "That's why I'd like to offer a bargain."

"I'm all ears," Lucian said, whistling "Who's Afraid of the Big Bad Wolf."

"You want intel, and I know everything there is to know about the inner workings of the Resistance," I said. "Release Eileen and I'll sing."

"Ah, but I already know those details," Lucian said with a cocky grin. "After all, I was part of the Resistance long before you were even on their radar."

"Yes, but you don't know everything," I said, watching his eyes carefully.

Zane cleared his throat. "Lucian, we're under strict orders—"

Lucian ignored him. "What don't I know?" he asked, taking my bait.

"You don't know that it was Eileen and me who infiltrated the Queen's Hive."

Lucian gave a start.

"Erik, don't do it!" Eileen said.

Lucian raised a hand in warning. "You're bluffing," he said.

"Am I? Shall I tell you what the Queen's throne looks like? Or about the goat-man that she killed?"

"I'm all ears, my friend," Lucian said, moving closer to me until he was an inch from my face.

"I'll tell you everything, but only if you let Eileen go," I promised. "Eileen can't tell you any more than me. Let her go—it will serve as a warning to the Resistance—and you can do whatever you like with me. It's a win-win for you."

"A win-win. I like the sound of that," Lucian mused with his head cocked back, his eyes staring at the ceiling contemplating. "Okay, I will consult my team. But you must understand. No matter how informative your information is, I will still be forced to torture you—even if we let Eileen dance away."

"I wouldn't expect less," I said.

Lucian gestured at Zane to follow him, then took several steps backwards and jaunted out the door.

Eileen and I had gained a momentary reprieve, but not for long.

CHAPTER 26
SACRIFICIAL LAMBS

"Well, there you have it. Now we can begin, my little sacrificial lambs."—Eichmann

"Erik, I won't let you sacrifice yourself for me," Eileen said the moment we were alone. "It won't help me or the movement."

"Listen, don't make me out to be a hero or anything," I said with a sneer, aware that we were being monitored and hoping Eileen would play along. "I want to get out of this as much as the next guy. If that means spilling my guts, I can live with that."

"You don't mean that! You can't!" Eileen cried, her eyes flashing.

"Obviously, you don't know me all that well, do you?" I said, trying hard to keep up the pretense and not cave to the disappointment in her eyes.

"I'm starting to wonder if I ever really knew you at all," Eileen said just as Lucian and Zane reappeared with a third person in tow, a tall, thin, balding man in a doctor's white examining coat.

A small woman entered the room last, her face covered with an operating mask, pushing a long operation room table. Strewn over the surface of the table were carpenters' tools: a hammer, pliers, screwdrivers, even long silver nails, among the other assorted tools.

This wasn't good.

I glanced over at Lucian to find him watching me closely, a small smile on his mouth and a devilish gleam in his eye. "The team appreciates your offer of assistance, but must graciously decline in order to pursue our original plan of action," he said, with a bow and a flourish of his hand.

"You don't have to do this, Lucian," I murmured urgently, hoping to find some trace of the old Lucian. "You can think for yourself. You don't have to be their slave."

"You know, Erik, that was the first great revelation I had when I converted," Lucian drawled. "Freedom IS slavery. Ignorance is strength. We were wrong all along, spouting all those platitudes about freedom and that sacrificial mumbo jumbo. It's a false promise."

"You can't mean that, Lucian," Eileen said, her eyes flashing. "I don't believe you could mean that."

"Oh, I believe it, sister dear," Lucian replied. "And soon you will, too."

"How can you live with yourself?" Eileen cried out. "You know what kinds of monsters these people are. You know what awful things they have done. Have you forgotten what they did to our parents?"

Lucian's eyes went cold, all pretense of congeniality gone. "I have forgotten nothing, but I have learned to look at things from a different perspective. You should do the same. Our parents were traitors to their government. You and Erik and the rest of the Resistance are traitors, as well."

"You're the traitor, Lucian!" I bucked against my restraints. "You're not converted. You're brainwashed, and you know it!"

"We're wasting time talking when action is so much more entertaining." Lucian glanced at me briefly, then looked away. "In any case, I'm just following orders and doing my job in the hopes of the betterment of humankind," he said. "Now we have dallied long enough. I leave you in the fastidious care of Dr. Eichmann."

With that, Lucian disappeared into the darkness of the outer room. There would be no further chance to keep him talking and delay the inevitable.

Zane cleared his throat to draw our attention. "Really," he said in his soft-spoken tone, "you should be appreciative of the great honor you're being given. Not everyone is privileged to have Dr. Albert Eichmann as their personal physician and conversion therapist."

"No offense, but this is an honor I could do without," I muttered.

"No offense taken," said Eichmann, stepping forward and temporarily blocking my view of Eileen. Up close, his large gray eyes were expressionless. Creeping purple veins lined his pale, white face. "However, we really should get on with the program."

"And what exactly is the program, if I might ask?" I ventured.

"Well, to put it bluntly, we're going to re-program you." Eichmann gestured to the nurse to wheel the table forward and stepped back, so Eileen and I could get a good glimpse of each other and his instruments of torture. "As you can see, we have an assortment of therapy tools to persuade even the most ardent of so-called freedom fighters."

"Our therapy has been quite successful," Zane added with a giggle. "All of Dr. Eichmann's patients—at least the ones who survived the reprogramming—have become valuable members of society."

"Well, there you have it. Now we can begin, my little sacrificial lambs," Eichmann said. He pressed a button on a handheld keyboard, causing my arms to slowly move upward and out. I saw my facsimile in Eileen, her arms splayed out, crucifixion-style.

Eileen cried out, fighting to resist the controls.

"What are you going to do?" I demanded of Eichmann. "At least have the decency to tell us."

"It's quite simple," he said. "You'll be asked a question. Your response will determine the measure of corrective therapy applied."

"Should we start with the fingernail stress test?" the nurse asked.

"Yes, that's a good introduction to the programming," Eichmann said, turning his attention back to me and Eileen. "A question will be posed. If you do not respond correctly, then I will begin to lift your fingernail from the flesh. It causes intense pain. Still, some of my more resistant patients have held out almost until the last fingernail," he smirked, shrugging his shoulders.

"There's no other alternative?" I pleaded.

"There really are no other alternatives," the doctor said. "So being a gentleman, we shall begin with the lady first."

"No!" I cried out. "Let me go first. I'll tell you what you want. I'll answer your questions."

"Sorry. I must do as ordered," Eichmann said with no emotion whatsoever. "Now we begin."

I watched in horror as Eichmann grabbed a thin pair of stiletto scissors. Facing Eileen, he said, "Your first question now. I warn you. Ponder your answers carefully."

"Nooooo!" I screamed.

"Shhhhh. Listen," Eichmann directed, glancing between Eileen and me. "There's always a price for freedom, but one must be willing to pay that price. Still, to show you that I am not an unreasonable man, I'll give you a choice. Are you willing, Eileen, to let your friend go first as he suggests and perhaps save yourself?"

"Yes! Do it, Eileen!" I begged.

Taking a deep breath, Eileen said quietly, "No, I won't do it. Do what you must."

"I'm disappointed in your response, Eileen," Eichmann uttered placidly. "You may, however, change your mind as the therapy progresses."

With that, Eichmann lifted Eileen's right hand, pulling it forward. He grabbed hold of her middle finger, bending it inward so that Eileen could see her fingernail. "Okay," he said, as he took the scalpel from the nurse's outstretched hand and slowly began lifting Eileen's fingernail. She screamed, her head tilted back towards the ceiling. Blood began to surface around the edges of the nail.

"Oh God, help me!" Eileen cried out.

"I will stop momentarily to let you reconsider your answers," Eichmann said calmly.

"If and when I get loose," I snarled, "I'm going to cut your sadistic throat, you maniac."

Eichmann ignored me. Moving closer to Eileen, he murmured, "Your answer, madam? Are you ready to let your associate take your place or do you want me to continue? I really don't think you'll last beyond a second or third finger nail removal."

Eileen began to whimper like a child. "No, I will not betray Erik."

"What follows is your decision," Eichmann said disapprovingly, "but maybe it's for the best." Then snatching a second finger, he again inserted his torture tool beneath her nail. Blood welled up and began dropping to the floor.

"Are you beginning to see the light?" he asked.

"I'll make you see the light, you monster," I growled, struggling to tear the restraints off my body and topple the table in the process.

Zane grabbed a taser and pointed it at me, warningly. "Don't make me use this on you, Erik."

Eichmann continued levering up Eileen's nail. Her eyes rolled back in her head. "Tsk, tsk, you really are not responding well to my therapy," Eichmann said.

"Stop, you're killing her!" I cried out.

That's when Eileen's face began to sparkle and glitter. She looked like a mosaic painting. I glanced down at my body. It looked as if I were becoming a mosaic piece of art, as well. I was breaking into minute, electromagnetic particles.

Eichmann's head swiveled back and forth between us. As comprehension dawned, he yelled to the nurse, "Alert! Alert! Something's going awry here. Call for assistance. Now!"

Those were the last words I heard before I fell into a tunnel of light. I was spinning and circling like the hands on an antique clock. A low buzzing noise filled my ears. I could see other human bodies ahead of me. They too were circling and floating down this weird tunnel.

Eileen's tortured face flashed before me like a scene from a horror movie. "Eileen, where are you?" I reached for her, but my hands and arms plunged into nothingness. Then everything went black. The tunnel of light had become a dark hole.

CHAPTER 27
BACK IN SUBTERRANEA

"What doesn't kill us makes us stronger."—Ginger

Slowly the darkness gave way to a bright light that dominated my vision.

"Erik, do you hear me?" A disembodied voice echoed in my mind. I tried to find the source of that voice, but all I saw were light and shadows. The voice faded in and out, repeating the question over and over again, until I finally mumbled a reply.

"Yes, I hear you," I whispered. "Where is Eileen?"

"Eileen is right here, beside you," the voice responded, clearer this time.

"Are you sure? Is she safe?" I asked, squinting against the light, almost able to make out the outlines of a man. "Where is here? What do you want?"

"It's okay. You're both safe now," the voice said. "You're back in Subterranea. Here, take a look." Someone approached and turned my head to the side.

Without the direct glare of the overhead light to contend with, I was able to see in greater detail.

I saw Eileen.

She lay unmoving on a hospital cot, her eyes closed and her head turned slightly in my direction. She appeared unharmed, except for one hand which was wrapped in gauze and the telltale bruises on her face from Lucian's blows.

"Eileen …" My voice broke as I whispered her name, the memory of her torture session flooding back in painful detail.

"Eileen is fine," the voice reassured me. "There will be no lasting damage."

I recognized the voice now. I turned and looked at Microwave Man, helmet and all, standing over me. "Frank!" I exclaimed, beyond glad to see a familiar face. "We were captured. They had us tied up. We couldn't get away."

"Looks like we got you out in the nick of time," Frank said, leaning down to peer into my eyes. "You haven't been here very long, though. Just long enough for Dr. Goode to give you a quick once-over and check your vitals." Frank gestured over his shoulder to a small, wiry woman hovering just behind him.

"We'll give you a more thorough examination later," Dr. Goode said. "For now, we're just glad you're back."

"But what happened?" I asked. "How did we get here? They were torturing Eileen. I couldn't stop them."

"The pain ended up working in your favor," Frank explained. "It reconnected Eileen to our destabilizing unit, which in turn connected us to you, too. So, in a sense, the pain was your savior."

"I don't get it," I said, trying to sit up. The doctor hovered at my side, monitoring the sensors attached to my arms and chest.

"Pain confers an intense electrical impulse," Frank said. "Your body is an electrical unit and its circuitry connects you to the cosmos. In a sense, you are a programmed unit. So we simply hacked into the program to destabilize your molecular structure."

"But how did you know it would work?" I asked.

"We didn't," Frank said with a shrug. "We were frantically trying to locate your signals. We didn't have a good lead on you until the torture began. That's when we flipped the switch to bring you back."

"Somehow, the Queen was able to sense us," I said. "We got away as quickly as we could, but the minute we got topside, it all went off kilter."

"You began stabilizing topside," Frank said. "That's when they grabbed you."

Eileen moaned quietly and began to move about restlessly. The doctor moved to her side.

"Erik?" Eileen cried out. "Where is Erik?"

"I'm here, Eileen," I said. "We're safe. You're safe."

She turned her head in my direction, squinting to see me, her big brown eyes filling with tears.

"Erik, I was so scared," she said, the tears slipping down her face.

"I was scared, too," I said, stretching out my hand to touch her and reassure myself that she was real and safe and there with me. "We're back in Subterranea. Frank and the team were able to locate and destabilize us just in time."

"I remember..." she murmured, glancing down at her hand. "Lucian...Lucian was there!"

"Lucian was there?" Frank echoed. "Did you talk to him? Was he hurt?"

"Oh, we talked to him all right," I said, anger bubbling up through my words. "He gave the go-ahead for Eileen to be tortured first."

"Lucian did what?" Ginger stepped into the room, a deadly gleam in his eyes.

"They turned him, Ginger," Eileen said, grief etched on her face. "He's not Lucian anymore."

Ginger moved to Eileen's side, rested a hip on the side of her cot, and with a gentleness that I'd never have guessed him capable of, reached out to stroke the bruises on her cheek.

"You walk into a wall?" he asked. "Or did Boy Wonder start throwing punches in the dark?"

Eileen looked away from him, unable to give voice to exactly how far Lucian had fallen.

"It was Lucian," I said flatly. "He had us strapped down on gurneys, slapped Eileen around for trying to reason with him, and then gave the order to have her tortured first."

Ginger nodded, glanced briefly at me, then asked the doctor how soon we could be released.

"Ginger," Frank interrupted. "These two are under medical care."

"They need at least a good 24 to 48 hours to recover," Doctor Goode confirmed. "The stress alone—"

"—was enough to kill them," Frank interrupted.

"Well, what doesn't kill us makes us stronger," Ginger said with a shrug, turning to leave. "They can have 24 hours to recover, not a minute more, and then Spidus needs to see them."

With Ginger gone, Dr. Goode and Frank tested us for any signs of cellular damage from the destabilization process and exposure to the radiation levels in the Queen's labs.

For the next 24 hours, Eileen and I alternated between medication-induced sleep to help us rest and recover and systemic flushes to rid our bodies of the toxins associated with destabilization.

We were together the whole time, which was fine by me. After all we'd been through together, after coming so close to losing one another, I wasn't ready to be apart even for a moment. Eileen seemed to feel the same way.

Strange to feel such tender emotions in the midst of such pain and horror, but I couldn't help it.

For the first time in my life, I was in love.

CHAPTER 28
MONSTERS WITHOUT
CONSCIENCES

"These old eyes have seen enough pain for many lifetimes. And still, it hurts to know that more pain will be inflicted before we can taste freedom again."—Spidus

Spidus wasted no time summoning us for our debriefing the moment Dr. Goode and Frank gave us the all-clear.

A new set of tubes had been inserted in Spidus' upper arms. One tube dangled down the side of his neck. Small drops of blood leaked onto the bed, creating an abstract, polka-dot pattern on the sheets.

"Good job, you two," Spidus said, looking weaker than ever. "You made it back intact."

"Just barely," I said, glancing at Eileen.

"Yes, but the risks proved worthwhile. You gave us some valuable insight to what the Controllers are up to," Spidus choked out in between coughing fits. Ginger hovered at his side, ever watchful.

"I just wish we'd been able to help Lucian in some way," Eileen said.

"That maniac is beyond help," Ginger snarled, never once looking away from Spidus.

"Maybe not," Spidus said. "Right now, however, our priority must be finding the Controllers' weak point and targeting it before they can undermine everything the Resistance has worked for. Lucian may actually help move us closer towards that objective."

"How?" I asked. "If you're thinking Lucian might be persuaded to work for our side again, I wouldn't bet on it. He's been totally rewired."

"I agree," Spidus said, pointing at the screen overhead. "Lucian has been on the rampage ever since you two slipped out of his grasp. He and his Werewolf Unit are wreaking havoc."

"Yep, they're searching for a fugitive and it's you," Ginger said with a sly grin. "Take a watch."

On the screen, the nightly news broadcast opened up with a breaking news story. "Authorities are in search of a dangerous criminal who is on the loose," announced the sculpted blonde anchor. "Wanted for robbery, murder and kidnapping, 19-year-old Erik Blair was last sighted near his old school, Academy Five."

"Me?" I sputtered. "I'm the criminal?"

After giving a brief rundown on me, the anchor passed the story off to a young man who was reporting live from Academy Five. Lucian, dressed in the black uniform of the Werewolf Units and leading a troupe in full body armor, strode down the steps of the Academy and stopped to speak with the reporter.

"The public should be on guard," Lucian warned, removing the helmet from his head and speaking into the microphone. "He is armed and dangerous. But we are doing all we can to capture him alive."

"How am *I* a dangerous criminal?" I asked, incredulous.

"Because the government says so and the media will report it unquestioningly," Spidus said. "That's all it takes for the masses to buy it lock, stock and barrel."

"Is it true that Blair is a member of the underground Resistance?" the reporter asked.

"Plenty of evidence points to that," Lucian said matter-of-factly, his deep set, black eyes emotionless, a scowl plastered across his face. "These terrorists are worse than cowards. They're scoundrels. Scum. They attack when our backs are turned."

"What are you doing to capture him, sir?" the reporter asked, waving his free hand in the air. "How do you plan to smoke him out?"

"I don't plan to smoke him out," Lucian said with a sneer. "He'll come to me."

Before the reporter could venture another question, Lucian grabbed the microphone and announced, "I have this directly from our President. I've been directed to challenge Mr. Blair to combat in the Queen's arena at the Celestial Bowl one week from today. If he can put me down—defeat me, that is—he can walk free and an automatic pardon will be granted to him and all members of the Resistance and those within the F-zones."

"Combat in the Celestial Bowl? A fight to the death? Full pardon for all Resistance fighters and unsavories?" the reporter squawked. "This is truly momentous, Mr. Freud. And what an honor for you!"

"Congratulations, kid," Ginger crowed. "Not even a month with the Resistance, and you're not just criminal number one, but you're about to star in your own reality show!"

"It is always an honor to serve our country," Lucian said, his face tightening up into a squint. "If Mr. Blair is a real patriot, he will prove it by meeting me at the Celestial Bowl. If the Resistance really cares about freedom for the masses, this is their chance to prove it."

"And if he doesn't show?" the reporter asked.

"Then he's not only a gutless coward but the Resistance itself will have been shown to be a sham," Lucian said. Handing the microphone to the reporter, Lucian smiled and walked away.

"There you have it," the reporter said. "We'll have to wait and see if Erik Blair, a man high on the wanted list, will dare to show his face. We'll be there and I know most of our audience will be, too. This is a major development, folks, and you heard it first right here. Back to you in the studios, Marlene."

Ginger switched off the transmission.

Spidus cleared his throat. "Lucian is putting you on notice, Erik," he said quietly. "He's throwing down the gauntlet. He knows we're watching."

"He's just trying to draw Erik out," Eileen said. "It's a trap!"

"It *is* a trap," Spidus acknowledged, "but it's a cleverly baited trap. And one we may not be able to resist."

"But if we know it's a trap, won't everyone else know it, too?" I asked.

"The masses live for bread and circuses," said Ginger.

"This is just a modern-day Roman arena and you are being thrown to the lions for the crowd's amusement and entertainment," Spidus explained. "They may suspect it's all a game—they may even know it's a sham—but they will tune in anyhow, and they will clamor for blood. What the Controllers have created are monsters without consciences: heartless human machines who are more concerned with watching television than helping their fellow human beings."

"He doesn't need to do this, Spidus," Eileen said, ready to fight. "There has to be another way."

"They've committed to the spectacle," Ginger interjected. "It's the best shot we're going to get at an audience like this. It may be our only chance to wake people up and tear back the curtain on the Controllers' freak show."

Spidus looked at Eileen and reached out to hold her hand. "These old eyes have seen enough pain for many lifetimes," he said. "And still, it hurts to know that more pain will be inflicted before we can taste freedom again."

"Which brings us to the big question," Ginger said. "Are you ready to meet Lucian head on?"

"Yes," I said, taking a deep breath. "I'll do it. I'm ready!"

"No, he's not!" Eileen countered forcefully.

"No, he's not," Spidus echoed, his voice almost an unrecognizable wheeze. "He's not ready, but he will be."

"We've got a week to prepare," Ginger said. "Piece of cake."

"Stop being so flippant," Eileen shot back, her eyes flashing a warning at Ginger. Turning to me, she said, "I don't like the sound of this. But if you're determined to risk your life, then we're going to make sure you're ready for whatever's going to be in that arena. And you'll have backup. Whatever you do, we do together. And I'm not budging," she declared, with a defiant glare that encompassed the three of us.

"Ginger will get a message to Lucian that you have accepted the challenge and that Eileen will be your second-in-command," Spidus said, his voice sounding stronger and more energized. "Everything we do from here on out has to be done with careful deliberation. The future of the Resistance depends on it."

CHAPTER 29
STRATEGY. HEART.
KNOWLEDGE.

"They don't want human beings. They want machines. Why? A machine does as it is programmed to do. It will smash. It will kill. It will obey the Demon. It will not speak out of turn. Hear me! Anyone, hear me! It's rebellion of any kind they fear the most. Why? It's rebellion that makes us truly human. Otherwise, we're no better than the monstrous robots that rule over us."—The Manuscript

"These two will need some sessions with Artemis," Ginger said, pulling out his handheld and sending out a coded message.

"Artemis?" I asked. "Who's Artemis?"

"Artemis Crockett will be your trainer in the martial art of gouge and bite," Spidus explained.

Eileen shook her head wearily.

"Say my name and you'll know who to blame," a gravelly voice said behind me.

"Artemis, you move fast," Ginger said. "You're going to need to work miracles with this one."

"So you're the sacrificial lamb, eh?" Artemis asked, reaching out and giving me a bone-rattling handshake. He sported a coonskin hat and a plasticine leather shirt, pants and moccasins.

"Looks like I'll need all the help you can give," I said.

"He needs some intensive training, Artemis," Ginger said. "He's going up against Lucian next week. Lucian's been turned."

"Yeah, I heard about that," Artemis said, shooting a look of sympathy at Eileen. "You holding up okay, doll face?"

"I'm holding up enough for what needs to be done," Eileen responded. "And I'm going to be training with you, too. I'm Erik's second."

Artemis nodded and turned to me. "I taught Lucian when he was with the Resistance," Artemis mused, placing his hand under his chin. "He was a fast learner."

"Erik will have to be a faster learner, then," Spidus declared.

Ginger's handheld crackled a message. After reviewing it, he leaned down to whisper to Spidus.

"Looks like we'll get a chance to see what Lucian has been learning," Spidus said, directing Ginger to send a transmission to the screens overhead. "Seems that Lucian is squaring off in Times Square with Otto."

"Wait," I said. "You mean that mental case who's always attacking the cops?"

"Ginger, roll the film," Spidus replied. Ginger turned and pointed his remote at the screen.

"Here goes," Ginger said as the screen lit up and revealed a teeming crowd surrounded by flashing electronic advertisements lining the buildings. "There. See that circled area surrounded by the guys dressed in Nazi-style outfits?"

In a small area, dark-clad, highly armed cops surrounded two guys moving to and fro as they faced each other. A Rex 84 patrolled behind them. The crowd watched, some standing on tables to take in the action.

"Zoom in," I directed Ginger, who gave me a curt glance over his shoulder.

There he was, the new Lucian, with knees bent facing his opponent, a tall, muscled brute.

"Watch Lucian's style of fighting and learn," Artemis said, eyes glued to the screen.

Otto growled, grunted and hunched over like a deranged gorilla. In bulk alone, he outweighed Lucian three times over. But Lucian didn't seem the least bit intimidated. In fact, Lucian appeared positively gleeful as he charged Otto, leaped and straddled him around the waist.

Pulling himself up to Otto's neck with one hand, Lucian used his other hand to pluck the man's eye from his skull and hold it up to an uproarious chorus of screams from the on-watchers. It happened that quickly.

The giant screamed in pain and bucked Lucian off him.

Lucian dropped to the ground. Then with a flourish, Lucian flashed a sword-like object, seemingly from out of nowhere, jumped between Otto's legs and rammed the sword into the giant's testicles.

Howling like a wounded dog, Otto stumbled into the crowd and collapsed.

Again, the crowd cheered.

Lucian took a bow, then turned and disappeared into the crowd.

No one said a word for several minutes after the screen went dark. This is who I had to face off against in a week?

"Lucian wanted you to see this, Erik," Spidus said, clearing his throat. "He's trying to intimidate you."

"He's also trying to intimidate anyone who wants to align with the Resistance," added Eileen.

"Well, it worked," I said with a gulp.

Artemis pounded me on the back. "Good man," he said. "You'd be a fool to not be intimidated by that butchery."

"Yeah, but I'd prefer not to be a dead fool," I said, the vision of Lucian re-playing in my head.

"You changing your mind, Boy Wonder?" Ginger asked, glancing at me sideways, a clear challenge in his voice.

"There's no shame in that," Eileen said, poking Ginger in the side.

"No, I'm not changing my mind," I said. "Besides, what can I lose at this point?"

"Your life. That's what you stand to lose, Erik," Eileen said, giving me an irritated stare. "I've already lost Lucian. I don't want to lose you, too."

"I know my limits, and there's no way I can learn enough—no matter how hard I train—to out-brutalize Lucian. I'm not a killer, and I'm not going to kill Lucian."

"Strategy, then," Artemis decreed abruptly. "Good plan. I'll start working on some tactics." With a nod to Spidus, he left as suddenly as he'd appeared.

"Strategy, heart and knowledge," Spidus declared, repeating the mantra he had spouted at me during one of our first meetings. "Yes … Ginger, get me the manuscript Erik found."

Upon being handed the sheaf of papers, Spidus leafed through them until he came to the page he wanted. "Eileen, read this one short passage."

Eileen pulled the page and read aloud:

Now is not the time to cut and run or, worse, do nothing. If I did, I couldn't live with myself. I can't spend my life crawling down in the hole every time one of those bastards emerges to kill, chase or challenge somebody. When I look into the eyes of children, I see death. The maniacs who control us don't want human beings. They want machines programmed to follow orders. Machines will smash. They will kill. They will blindly obey. It's rebellion they fear. We must rebel. The people must remember what it is to want freedom.

"Guerilla tactics. Rebellion. Humanity. Compassion. Individuality. Independence," Spidus said. "Focus on these, Erik. That is how you will defeat Lucian and wake people up so they can see what a hell—what a prison—we're all living in. Only then do we have a chance of changing things for the better."

CHAPTER 30
WINNING BY WHATEVER
MEANS POSSIBLE

"The quest for freedom—the hunger to live a life that is one's own—the need to feel something other than fear: that must be greater than any one individual. That is not something I can generate. We must each come to that place of understanding for ourselves."—Spidus

No matter how much I wanted to *not* kill Lucian, I also had to make sure he didn't succeed in killing me. So the next day, I had my first lesson in the art of gouge and bite.

It was not a pretty sight.

Artemis didn't pull any punches. Unfortunately, I was so busy trying to avoid *being* punched that I failed to land any punches.

"Stop fighting defensively," Artemis shouted. "You want to get yourself killed? Lucian will not hesitate to go for the kill."

"He doesn't hate you enough, Artemis," Ginger observed, while lounging by the sidelines. "The boy's got no fire in him. He needs a better motivator."

"You volunteering?" Artemis asked Ginger, dodging my punch only to duck and kick my feet out from under me.

"Why not? I haven't done any real damage to anyone in a while," Ginger said lazily. He stretched his neck, jogged in place and removed his various communication devices. "I don't want to get rusty."

Ginger moved in on me before Artemis had even finished making my head spin. If Artemis was a demanding opponent, Ginger was downright nasty. Before long, he had me forgetting it was an exercise bout. All I wanted to do was wipe the floor with him. By the end of the session, we were both panting hard and bleeding profusely.

I was black and blue and aching all over by the next day. Eileen, determined to be my second, trained just as hard and took as many hits as I did. She didn't need Ginger's "help" to tap into her anger, though. She just pictured what they'd done to Lucian and she was ready to tear the Queen's head off.

On the third day, Eileen and I met Artemis in a small roped-off arena. He was again dressed in a plastic, faux leather outfit.

"Getting right down to business," he said, pondering the floor. "You've already been trained in basic martial arts, which in an ordinary fight would be fine. But facing off with Lucian will require a whole different attitude on your part."

"What kind of attitude?" I asked. "I already said I'm not going to kill Lucian."

"You may not have a choice," Artemis growled. "You're not fighting your old schoolmate. You're facing off against a killer who has been created for one thing only: to put an end to you. Lucian's empathetic nervous system has been disconnected. He will have no feelings and no sympathy for you, even as his opponent. His only goal is to win by whatever means possible."

"And my goal is to not kill or be killed," I said. "Which leaves us at something of a stalemate."

"That's no stalemate," Artemis replied. "That's a suicide mission."

"Erik, Artemis is right," Eileen chimed in, an intense look of concentration on her face. "It's not enough to avoid being killed. You're going to need some offensive techniques under your belt."

"I will not kill Lucian," I repeated.

"I don't want you to kill him, either," Eileen said. "But you're going to have to reconcile yourself to subduing him—even hurting him—in order to get out of that arena alive. If only there were a way to make it *look* like you'd killed him, without really killing him ..."

"I don't know about all that," Artemis muttered, "but I know that Spidus wants you to get some basic training in the gouge and bite method of hand-to-hand combat, and that's what we're going to do."

"So I'm to get as low or lower as the bastard I'm up against?" I emphasized.

"It's that or have your eyes plucked out, your testicles torn apart or your guts ripped from your midsection," Artemis said matter-of-factly. "We'll start with a video tutorial," he instructed, pointing to a screen on the wall.

It looked like a scene from a badly filmed movie. One guy was astraddle another who was squirming and kicking his legs. The guy on top suddenly thrust his thumbs into the other guy's eye socket and wiggled it repeatedly while the victim screamed, trying to get free. Then slowly the victim on the mat went limp as the attacker jumped up and claimed victory over the dead man at his feet.

"No way in the world am I going to do that to someone, let alone Lucian," I declared.

"Well, then you're gonna lose and so will that kid who's betting his life on you," Artemis said.

"What kid?" Eileen asked. "What are you talking about?"

"Unknown to the public who sits and worships during these bouts, there's a prize for the Queen and her so-called Knights of Darkness," Artemis said. "If you lose and Lucian wins, a sacrifice must be made to Ghello."

"They're going to sacrifice a child?" Eileen asked, looking intently at Artemis.

"A child, one of the hybrids, I believe, will be turned loose and hunted."

"Spidus knows about this?" I asked.

"He asked me to warn you. From what we know, the sacrificial victim is a chimera, part goat, part human. A goat child," Artemis explained.

Eileen and I looked at each other.

"Right," I said with a sigh. "So not only do I need to not kill Lucian or be killed and/or maimed by him, but I also need to figure out a way to reverse whatever they've done to him, inspire the F-Zoners and Resistance fighters, and save the chimera. Anything else?"

"That about covers it," Artemis said with a rueful smile.

From that point onwards, the week was a blur of combat training, strategy sessions and war councils to ensure that while I was distracting the Controllers and the masses and hopefully setting a rebellion in motion, the Resistance would be chopping at the roots of the evil empire.

What few, meager moments we had left over were all that could be spared for sleep and recovery. Even then, Eileen and I were rarely alone. Certainly, there was no time to explore my new-found feelings for her or wonder if she felt something for me, something more than brotherly affection. There was a moment or two, at least, when I could have sworn I saw something in her eyes, but she didn't speak up, so I stayed quiet, too.

After all, what kind of prospect was I? A guy on his way to kill or be killed by her brother. Even if I succeeded in staying alive and somehow rescuing Lucian, there was no way I could avoid hurting him. Or vice versa.

Finally, after endless days of practicing how to outmaneuver, overpower and overcome someone intent on inflicting the utmost amount of pain in the shortest amount of time, Artemis declared us ready. Or at least as ready as we could be in a week's time.

Ginger had continued to serve as my sparring partner. Incredibly, after pummeling me and being pummeled by me, he seemed to have developed what I would almost call an affection for me. Almost.

Leaving Artemis' training arena, Eileen and I tried to sneak away long enough to have a few minutes alone, but Ginger—always on the prowl—nipped that in the bud.

"You're not under the impression that you're done with your training, are you?" Ginger growled. "You do realize that Lucian will be training round the clock, right? And that you've got less than 36 hours to cram in whatever else those little noggins of yours can hold?"

"We're calling it a day," I said, glancing over at Eileen, who looked as exhausted as I felt. "We've done all we can to prepare."

"Why don't you let Spidus be the judge of that?" Ginger said, mockingly. "He's waiting to see you in his chambers."

Spidus' room appeared darker than usual as we approached his bed. A man in a white coat was injecting a needle in Spidus' arm. He appeared to be sleeping.

"We're here, Spidus," Eileen said softly as we stood by the bed. His eyes remained closed.

"I know," Spidus said, struggling to breathe. "I don't need to see you to sense your presence."

"Are you dying, Spidus?" I asked, earning myself a kick in the shin from Ginger and a warning frown from Eileen.

"We're all dying, Erik," Spidus replied, a small smile playing across his mouth. "Some of us are just dying at a faster rate."

"What I really meant to say is that you can't die, Spidus," I said, stumbling over my words. "You're the key to the Resistance movement. If you go down, the movement will crumble."

"It will only crumble if the people in the movement stop caring. If I die, will you stop believing in freedom?" he asked, this time opening his eyes and staring at me intently.

"No, of course not, but ..."

"The quest for freedom—the hunger to live a life that is one's own—the need to feel something other than fear: that must be greater than any one individual," Spidus said. "That is not something I can generate. We must each come to that place of understanding for ourselves."

Ginger cleared his throat to interrupt us. "Aldous is here, Spidus."

A tall guy in a white jumpsuit with big, black goggles over his eyes entered the room. "As requested, I have the disc with the complete layout of the Celestial Bowl arena," the man said in a clipped, robotic voice. He moved like an automaton. Handing the disc to Ginger, Aldous did a silent about-face, clicked his heels together and walked away.

The disc contained the arena layout and the field where the big game was played. Ginger showed us the smaller arena where I would be facing off with Lucian. It was to be located in the center of the field.

I didn't say anything, but I knew those fields well enough, having watched the Celestial Bowl games for years. That's what we were programmed to do, after all. What used to be entertaining, however, now looked hideous to me.

"Are you ready for your match, Erik?" Spidus asked, his voice growing a bit weaker.

"As ready as I can be," I said. "I still don't know if I can be a monster like Lucian, or if I even want to be."

"I believe that's your strength, son," Spidus replied. "Play to it. Being truly human is the only way to really live. Otherwise, you're just surviving." Spidus shook his head slowly and seemed to drop off into a deep sleep.

"I still think there's something to be said for surviving," Ginger muttered, looking with concern at Spidus' flagging energy. "Anyhow, Spidus needs some rest and so do you guys. Match Day will be here faster than you think."

I reached out and touched Spidus' shoulder, trying to transfer some small spark of my life force to him. Ginger gave me a quiet look of understanding, before turning to gaze down at Spidus.

No matter what Spidus said about the Resistance being larger than just him, I didn't want to think of how lost—and leaderless—we would be were anything to happen to him.

CHAPTER 31
THE STAR-SPANGLED
CROSS

"Time is your ally. You have the power to change the past, present and future if you are willing to live and die in the moment."—Narcissus

"Looks like we've got ourselves a media star," Ginger said, pointing to the screen in the control room.

"Enemy of the state to do battle with federal agent!" blared the headline, which accompanied a picture of me full screen.

"That should pull in the ratings," Ginger remarked, patting me on the back. "Good versus evil makes for great entertainment."

The onscreen news anchor, some guy with a perpetual smile plastered on his face, gave the highlights of the upcoming showdown. "Erik Blair, a former Academy Five student gone bad, is fomenting rebellion. His opponent, Lucian Freud, once a fellow student and now an impressive fighter, is championing the people's right to law and order. This should be something! So tune in folks! You don't want to miss this one!"

"I wish *I* could miss this one," I muttered.

Eileen patted me on the shoulder. "I wish you could, too," she said.

"Well, here's one you probably don't want to miss," Ginger said. "Malkin, the Queen's right hand confidant, has requested a private meeting with you tomorrow afternoon before the match."

"Malkin wants a private meeting with me?" I glanced over at Eileen. This didn't sound good. "What for?"

Ginger shrugged. "Your guess is as good as anyone else's," he said.

"Should we risk it?" Eileen asked. "What if it's a trap?"

"They're spending way too much time building up the excitement for this match," Ginger said. "They're not going to disappoint the masses. In any case, we don't have much of a choice. Malkin's bodyguards will meet us at the Violence Reduction Center at Seventh and Broadway. From there, we'll be escorted to meet with the Queen's man. That's where we'll part ways. After the meeting, you two will be taken to the arena."

"What about you?" I asked.

"I'll be in position waiting," Ginger said. "We've got a few surprises of our own planned for tomorrow. For today, however, we want you and Eileen to run through some last-minute scrimmage plays while you're in costume."

"Why do we have to wear a costume, anyhow?" I grimaced. "Isn't it enough that I'm prepared to take on a maniac on national television?"

"Image is everything, my boy," Ginger responded with a grin, pulling out two packages and handing one to each of us. "We've retrofitted the costumes to make them more useful in the arena. For one thing, they're tight-fitting and slick, which will make it harder for Lucian to grab hold of you too easily. You can try them on after your meeting with Narcissus."

"*Another* meeting," I grumbled.

"Narcissus requested the meeting," Ginger said. "And Spidus thought it might be helpful."

"And who is this person, exactly?" I asked.

"Narcissus is indescribable," Eileen laughed. "Trust me, you want to meet him. He sees the shadow people."

"Of course he does," I said, shaking my head and glancing at Ginger, who was smirking as usual.

"No, really. According to Narcissus, the shadow people are visionaries from the future. They see things that have already happened," Eileen explained. "Narcissus uses what they tell him to predict the future."

With Ginger taking the lead as usual, we navigated our way through the maze of tunnels that ran through Subterranea until we arrived at the entrance to Narcissus' sanctuary.

Narcissus' chamber looked like it belonged in a museum catalogue. Sprinkled about on the walls were mirrors of every size, shape and style. Decorative chairs and tables with semi-melted candles were scattered here and there.

Narcissus glided across the floor towards us, dressed like a swami, his head covered in a black bandanna with gold stars. He was dressed in a matching black robe.

"Our new gladiator," he said by way of a greeting. "And you bring the warrior and the maiden."

"I'll leave them with you, then," Ginger said, clearly anxious to be on his way.

"No, stay," Narcissus ordered. "This concerns you, as well."

"Have you had a vision about the match?" Eileen asked.

"I have had a vision, but how it pertains to the match only you will know," he said, looking directly at me. "Step over here."

The three of us stepped forward as he turned and looked into a large circular mirror located behind him. I could see all four of us reflected in the mirror: two warriors, a maiden, and a mage.

"Our images will soon dissipate," Narcissus informed us. "In their place, you will see images of those who know, those who see. Watch the mirror, please."

Gradually, our images in the mirror grew grainy and disappeared.

Narcissus spoke to the mirror. "Venus, are you there?"

At his words, the mirror grew hazy and then a beautiful face appeared. The image rippled and flowed across the glass as if the entire surface had been turned to water. The woman's lips moved, but no sound came forth.

"What can you tell me about my friends here?" Narcissus asked.

Venus' eyes moved from Eileen to Ginger and then me. When she got to me, she jerked back with a look of horror, and spoke to Narcissus once again, her lips moving rapidly but no sound coming forth that we could hear. Suddenly, she stopped moving, her image disappeared and the mirror resumed its reflection of our four faces.

"Venus brings dire warnings, my friends," Narcissus said. "The enemy is waiting. A trap has been set."

"What kind of a trap?" Eileen asked.

"The vision I saw earlier showed a Roman arena," Narcissus recounted, his eyes closed. "Standing in the middle of the arena is a wooden cross. Flags—stars and stripes—were sprinkled about."

"A star-spangled cross?" Ginger smirked.

"You are to be a blood sacrifice," intoned Narcissus. "You are to be sacrificed as an atonement for the sins of society."

"Sacrificed how exactly?" I asked, my stomach doing flip flops.

"I see you nailed to that cross—pain, blood and guts on display for all to see," the swami replied.

"Is that all?" Eileen asked.

"Isn't that enough?" I murmured. Eileen nudged me to silence.

"That was my vision," Narcissus explained, opening his eyes and looking at me. "But Venus also had some words for you."

"This should be good," Ginger cackled, earning himself a reproving frown from Eileen.

"Venus said that time is your ally," Narcissus explained. "You have the power to change the past, present and future if you are willing to live and die in the moment."

"I don't get it," I said.

"Neither do I," said Eileen.

"That makes three of us," Ginger chimed in.

"You have a decision to make," Narcissus said, placing his hand on my shoulder and leading us out of his chamber. "Time can be altered. The power is in your hands. The decision is yours. No one can decide for you. And no one else can live this moment for you. You can change the future by changing the past. The foundation stones have already been laid."

"Does Spidus know about this?" I asked.

"Spidus knows many things," Narcissus replied obliquely. "You have only to ask."

Spidus did indeed know many things.

When we later asked him about Narcissus' vision of the cross in the arena, he shrugged. "They're bringing the past forward. In the days of

Roman tyranny, the cross sent a strong warning to those who persisted in their struggle for freedom."

"So what's the plan?" I asked. "How do we avoid death by crucifixion?"

"Again, I don't know," Spidus replied. "The early Christians refused to be party to the Roman spectacle: they opted not to fight back. It was not what the cheering, jeering crowds expected. They wanted a blood-and-guts, to-the-death battle and all they got was a chance to see some beasts feast on unresisting victims. It didn't make for much of a show."

"We've gone back to the Roman games again?" I asked, nonplussed.

"No, we're not back to Rome," Spidus said, this time with renewed energy. "Rome has come forward to us. Time is relative. Venus is right."

"Spidus, you've got to give me something to go on, because I'm lost at sea," I said, glancing helplessly at Eileen. Ginger shot me a rare look of sympathy.

"We may all come on different ships, but we're in the same boat now," Spidus said. "One of my heroes said that, and he was right about that and so many other things."

I stared at Spidus, dumbfounded. Was he losing his mind?

"No, I'm not losing my mind," Spidus said with a smile. "This is your journey, Erik. Yours and no one else's. It started long before you picked up that manuscript and where it will end depends on you. We will be with you, always, in one way or another, but you're the one who must face Lucian in that arena. It's down to you and only you."

"I don't know if I can do this, Spidus," I said. "I mean, yeah, I can face off against Lucian. But I'm no hero. And I'm no leader. And I definitely have no idea what it is you're trying to tell me right now."

"When the time is right, you'll understand," Spidus said. "Just remember this: a man who won't die for something is not fit to live."

CHAPTER 32
THE BLACK IRON PRISON

"The hunt must go on."—Malkin

Match Day dawned after a night of fitful dreams in which I saw myself being crucified over and over again by a man with my face.

By the time we had woken, dressed, eaten and had our final pow wow with Spidus, Eileen and I were both a basket of nerves. For all his bravado, Ginger wasn't in any better shape.

Good to his word, he accompanied us through the catacomb mazes of Subterranea, up a winding stairway, and out onto a grassy knoll topside, where the brown hazy air mingled with the scents of carnival food—popcorn, hot dogs and funnel cakes—being offered up for the festivities.

"Here. Wear this," Ginger said, handing me a low-slung black visor cap. "Your face is too recognizable now. We don't want to be intercepted before we reach the Black Iron Prison."

"I thought we were meeting Malkin at the Violence Reduction Center?" Eileen asked. "Isn't Black Iron his private residence?"

"Change of plans," Ginger said, sidestepping a couple of F-zoners who had passed out on the grass and pointing up a long incline. "Malkin's prison palace is located across the street from the Strawberry Fields park."

We walked across a large circular paved area. Embedded in the ground was a single word: "Imagine."

"Imagine what?" I asked.

"Imagine living in a world without tyrants, violence, pain, fear," Eileen replied. "Imagine living in peace."

"Imagine if we could actually spend ten minutes together without you two polluting the air with endless talk," Ginger muttered, gesturing for us to follow him across the street to a black cubicle. It was perched on a corner across a busy street.

Driverless cars swiped by in a blur. "Don't make eye contact with anyone passing by, and whatever you do, don't go near the Atlas Fours strutting back and forth."

The androids were crisscrossing in front of the black cube. Dark-clad armed guards stood poised to repel any intruders. One of the androids zeroed in on a guy walking past who had stopped to peer into the cubicle. It gave the guy a shove to get him moving. He scurried away.

As we walked up to one of the helmeted guards, Ginger announced, "These two have a meeting with Malkin."

"ID confirmation?" the guard asked, slipping the eye shield up on his helmet and giving me a quizzical stare. His eyes were the same dark, dead, obsidian black as Lucian's.

I stepped forward as the dark-clad storm trooper ran a scanner on my iris, then on Eileen.

"Confirmed," he said. "Pass through."

"I'll see you on the other side," Ginger said, giving Eileen a half-hug and slamming his hand down on my back. "You remember what we taught you and don't let your guard down for any reason. From here, you'll be escorted straight to the arena. If anything goes awry, you know what to do."

That was the last we saw of Ginger.

We walked through the metal doors, unsure of what awaited us. Another armed, helmeted guard waited for us inside. After running our biometrics through yet another security scanner, he signaled for us to follow him.

We trekked down a brightly lit, narrow hallway with stark black walls.

"Wait here," the guard ordered, as he pushed a large red button by a wide silver door located at the end of the hallway. The door swung open.

"Wait there," the guard ordered, directing us to two gold ornamental armchairs. "I'll inform Lord Malkin you're here," he said. He disappeared through the silver doors.

We sat in silence for several minutes, occasionally glancing at each other as strange, rotating surveillance cameras peered down at us from the walls.

Figuring this might be the last chance I had to tell Eileen how I felt about her, I grabbed her hand. The guard walked back in before I could utter a word.

"Lord Malkin will see you now."

We were ushered into a large rectangular room with a low ceiling. The room was dominated by a stainless-steel metal throne at its far end. Two more guards stood motionless on either side of the throne. Their eyes stared straight ahead. "Wait here," our escort told us as he turned and walked out of the room.

"Erik! Eileen!" I heard a voice exclaim from the side. Approaching us was the tall thin guy with the long black ponytail we had seen in the Queen's throne room. He was dressed in a dingy gray t-shirt and blue jeans. "I'm Lord Malkin, but you can call me Randal," he said with a smile, thrusting his hand forward.

"You're Malkin? The Queen's advisor?" I asked, shaking the offered hand.

"Yes," he said with a congenial smile. "Don't mind the clothes. I try to be informal when at home."

"I'm sure you're wondering why I asked you here today, before the Big Match," he said. Eileen glanced over at me and shrugged her shoulders. "Our corporate advisory council is very pleased. According to Control Central, the media is going bonkers over your bout with Lucian."

"They're pleased?" I asked incredulously.

"Of course," Malkin trilled. "This Match will really ramp up the ratings. They've been slipping lately. Nothing like a good, bloody fight to the death to make the masses feel patriotic."

Malkin turned and gestured for us to follow him to a closet. "We can continue talking while I get dressed," he said, slipping on a dark ornamental robe that touched the floor. "As you'll see, we take our business very seriously."

"So why have we been invited to see you?" Eileen asked.

"Obviously, we want this to go well," Malkin replied. "The ad revenue alone is crashing out of the ceiling. That's what happens when you work together. I think we could turn this into a lucrative commercial venture for the government interests and the Resistance, if we script it just right."

"You want to work together to make money?" I asked.

"Of course. Isn't that the point?" Malkin tittered. "These citizen against citizen extravaganzas—whether it's election politics, sport extravaganzas and so on—are great distractions and the masses just lap them up. It also makes them so much easier to control."

"Why are you telling us this?" Eileen asked, her eyes narrowed in warning.

"I'm trying to make you an offer you can't refuse," Malkin said, glancing slyly at me.

"So this is a negotiation?" I asked.

"Not exactly," Malkin said with a careless shrug. "More a clarification of terms."

"And what terms are you clarifying, exactly?" Eileen asked, pointedly.

Malkin took a step back and cleared his throat. "Lucian wants to rip your head off. He's not going to back down for any reason. And he will not show you any mercy. But…"

Malkin let the sentence trail off, baiting us into asking him to continue.

We remained silent.

When it became apparent that we would not be playing his mind games, he pouted, sneered and sniffed derisively.

"Lucian will show no mercy," he repeated, "but we have our own means of ensuring the outcome we desire. Now if we could somehow come to an understanding, I could arrange for you to be the victor of today's games."

"Interesting proposition," I replied, playing along. "And you would do this how exactly?"

Malkin's eyes gleamed with the ferocity of a feral cat about to pounce. "Lucian can be re-programmed to self-destruct at your hands," he purred. "It wouldn't take much for you to overpower him in such a state. And then you'd be the hero of the hour, wouldn't you?"

"Which means the Resistance wins and its fighters would get cleared," Eileen said, watching Malkin intently. "That's a big boost for the Resistance, so what's in it for you?"

Malkin remained silent, a ghost of a smile flitting over his face.

"He wants to co-opt the Resistance," I said, suddenly understanding what this whole meeting was about. "If I lose, the status quo remains: the Resistance will keep fighting and the Controllers will have to fight on two fronts to maintain power."

"And if you win, that's a big boost to the Resistance," Eileen added. Turning to Malkin, she continued, "But if the Controllers turn Erik into their poster child, their freedom fighter, they can use Erik to persuade the people that things are going to be fine, that it's just a bunch of creeps hiding in Subterranea, out to cause trouble. That way, the Controllers look even better."

Malkin buffed his nails on his robe. "You're smarter than we expected, I'll give you that."

"And the hunt?" I asked. "What happens to the goat child?"

"Ah, so you know about the hunt, do you? Well, that's a different matter," Malkin said dispassionately, raising his eyebrows as his face shapeshifted to that of a lime green lizard. Scales appeared on its surface, and then just as quickly disappeared. "The hunt must go on."

"Thanks for the offer," I said, watching him shift from lizard to human again in the blink of an eye. "but I'll take my chances in the arena."

"Your chances are slim," Malkin replied, grabbing hold of a long metal staff and pounding it on the floor. "Guards, escort these two to the arena. It's time for the show to begin!"

Two guards frogmarched us out of the Black Iron Prison and into a heavily armored police van.

Eileen gave me a signal to keep quiet. I did as I was told. Lights flashing and sirens blaring, the van sped us to our destination.

Blinking electronic signs lined the buildings, advertising the Celestial Bowl. Guards were lined up three deep in front of the stadium.

We came to a halt at a side entrance.

Two guards wearing black face masks and carrying mini-cannons escorted us from the car into the arena. We entered the stadium from a side entrance and stepped into a heavily guarded elevator.

From there, it was a quick ride up to a private level suite reserved for VIPs that looked like some rich guy's penthouse living room. Paintings on the walls. Plush chairs. Lavish furnishings. A large picture window looked out on the stadium field below. And a French waiter hovering dutifully in the wings.

"Wait here until you're summoned," the guard said as he did an about-face, clicked his heels and left. "You've got 15 minutes until you have to be in the arena."

For the first time in what seemed like forever, it was just Eileen and me alone. As badly as I wanted a few minutes alone with her, suddenly, I was tongue-tied and unable to utter a single word.

"Here, take this," Eileen said, handing me a strange disk marked with some kind of hieroglyphic symbol.

"What is it?" I asked, turning it over to read the words etched into the back: "Love is the only force capable of transforming an enemy into a friend.-MLK"

"My dad gave this to me just before he died," Eileen said. "Lucian has one, too."

"What do the markings mean?" I asked, tilting it this way and that so that the light glinted off the lines etched deeply into its surface.

"The inverted Y with a line through it is a runic symbol for the death of man," she explained, reaching out to run a finger lightly over the markings on the disk's surface. "The circle around the inverted Y signifies the unborn child. Together, they stand for peace."

"The Controllers don't want peace and love," I said, glancing out into the mobbed arena.

"What do *you* want?" Eileen asked.

"I want to get out of this alive," I said with an apologetic shrug. "I'm no martyr, and I'm not ready to die. But I also don't want to kill Lucian or give him a chance to kill me. And if I do make it out of this alive, I want you and me to—"

"They're ready for you," a commanding voice said behind us.

"We'll be with you in a minute," Eileen said to the guard. "What were you saying, Erik?"

"Nothing that wouldn't be better said after this is all over," I said, reaching out to touch her cheek.

She grabbed hold of my hand and held it still against her cheek for a heartbeat. "I'm going to hold you to that," she said with a whisper. "Whatever happens down there, I want you to know that—"

Once again the guard interrupted. "We've got a schedule to keep. It's time to go."

"There's time enough for this," I said, reaching down to touch my lips to Eileen's as her eyes misted over with tears. "Now we can go."

CHAPTER 33
THE ARENA

"For a moment, I wished I could start over, turn back the clock to a time when I was still clueless, still self-absorbed, still oblivious to the menace of the shadow government."—Erik

Perhaps it was my dread of the inevitable confrontation with Lucian that seemed to make time speed up when I wanted so badly to slow everything down.

We descended to the arena level in a bright metallic elevator that was tricked out with every imaginable luxury. Even so, I felt like I had bought a one-way ticket to hell, with the Devil waiting somewhere right around the corner.

As we exited the elevator, another heavily armed guard approached us, flashed some credentials at our escort, and indicated wordlessly that he would be taking over and leading us into the arena.

Our new armed escort, his face obscured and covered from head to toe in combat gear, kept shooting me quick, covert glances, but otherwise, silence reigned as we made our way out of the elevator and through a jostling, raucous crowd.

Eileen kept pace with me, somber-eyed and watchful.

Without her by my side, her hand gripping mine, I'm not sure I would have had the strength or the courage to keep moving forward.

In this way, putting one foot in front of the other, looking neither right nor left, heads held high and hands clasped, we made our way through the labyrinth of corridors circling the arena.

We came to a halt at a small door just to the side of the arena entrance. Using his gun to direct us, the guard ushered us inside what appeared to be a grimy, grungy locker room, lined with rusty, dusty, dented lockers and scuffed, dusty benches. The room reeked of old sweat and dirty feet.

In the middle of the small room, a man—young and wiry, wearing the unofficial uniform of the techie (ear buds, crisp white shirt and battered jeans)—issued a series of orders into a small headset while typing frantically on a screen device. The ID tag hanging around his neck identified him as Jack Rael, television producer.

Disconnecting the call, Rael turned towards us, his hand extended for a brisk handshake. "We've got 15 minutes until the match starts. Let me explain a few of the ground rules," he said. "From start to finish, your segment will last 30 minutes with no commercial breaks."

"I didn't realize this was a timed match," I replied, nonplussed. "What if there is no winner by the 30-minute mark?"

"That's unlikely, but one way or another, there'll be a winner," Rael said, giving me a forced smile. "If you and Lucian are still alive and fighting by the time we reach the 30-minute mark, the fight will be extended by 3 minutes and the winner will be decided by an open vote."

"Who casts this open vote?" I asked, glancing quickly at Eileen.

"Viewers will have a chance to weigh in and vote: thumbs up you win or thumbs down you lose," Rael said.

"And what about Lucian?" Eileen asked.

"Lucian's fate is tied to Erik's fate," Rael said with a careless shrug. "One way or another, someone must die. If the audience selects Erik as the winner, then Lucian dies. If Lucian is declared the winner, then Erik dies."

"So the only way I can get out of this alive is for Lucian to die, either by my hand or the government's?" I asked.

"That about sums it up," Rael said, consulting his timer. "We're down to seven minutes before the bout starts. We'll need you in place in two minutes."

"Wait. Where do the seconds come in?" Eileen asked. "We were told each side had to have their own seconds."

"The match is being broadcast live, so it must run for 30 minutes," Rael said with exaggerated patience. "If it ends too prematurely, the seconds will be called in to continue fighting to fill up the air time."

"So this is all just a game for television ratings? You're just trying to entertain the public?" Sickened was a mild word for what I was feeling.

"What planet have you been living on?" Rael sneered. "It's all for the public's viewing pleasure, didn't you know? The people want entertainment. They want the thrill of a fight from the comfort of their living rooms. Our job is to give the people what they want."

"Get this straight: I'm not entering the arena just to make show and help you dupe the public," I growled. "Don't you care about what's happening to this country?"

"My job isn't to meddle in the government's business," Rael replied. "My job is to produce a television show that pulls in the ratings and keeps the audience in their chairs and tuned in. I'm just doing my job."

"I've heard that line before," Eileen muttered in disgust, glancing over at me, then back at Rael. "Who's serving as Lucian's second?"

Rael consulted his screen device. "Lucian will be backed up by Therian. He's a chimera."

"Another chimera?" I asked, taken aback.

"Yes. He's a reptilian-human hybrid," Rael said, flashing his screen device at us.

Therian stared back at us from Rael's screen device. Standing about seven feet tall, the chimera's head was a disconcerting combination of reptile and human. His mouth was hinged and lined with jagged teeth. His skin was scaly and light green. Long claws extended from his elongated fingers. His body was one huge mass of muscle. He looked a lot like the dead, bleeding creature Eileen and I had seen in the Violence Reduction Center.

"They've got an alligator man lined up as Lucian's second?" Eileen exclaimed, recoiling in horror.

"Should be great for a ratings spike, if we need it," Rael replied. "Anyhow, it's time for the show. The guard will escort you into the arena. I'll monitor from the sidelines."

It was a short trek to the arena. As we were nearing the opening to the arena, Eileen nudged me and pointed to a three-foot square cage a few feet in front of us. Crammed inside the cage, his head hanging down like someone on death row, was the goat child…the Queen's so-called bounty.

As we approached the cage, the little creature raised his head, looked us both in the eyes and cowered in fear. Tears filled his piercingly blue eyes.

Bending low to peer into the cage, Eileen murmured, "We won't hurt you. We're here to help. What is your name?"

"Altair," the small creature answered, shivering in terror. "My name is Altair. I don't want to die. Please don't let them kill me. They killed my father. I'm scared."

"Me too, kid," I said, furtively testing the lock on the cage door. "Don't give up, you hear me? Fight back if you need to and if you get the chance, run."

The guard cleared his throat in warning and nudged us to keep moving. With a defiant glance, Eileen reached into the cage, patted Altair on the cheek and squeezed his hand before walking with us towards the entrance for the staging ground for the fight.

Every step of the journey was inundated with a sensory overload of sounds and smells and sights. The rumble of the crowd. The salty aroma of popcorn. The burnt smell of grilling meat hawked by food vendors. The blinding glare from the spotlights. The dizzying array of products advertised on flashing billboards. The helmeted stormtroopers who lined the arena, guns held at attention. The pulsating digits of a countdown clock ticking down the seconds until match time.

It was a scene of mayhem and madness, and the clock served as a painful reminder that for 30 minutes, I would be at the center of the storm.

The guard—who had yet to utter a word and communicated only by gesturing with his gun—indicated that we would be walking the perimeter in order to take our places at the edge of the arena. A small ring, the kind you'd see in a boxing match, had been set up at the center of the arena.

Lucian lounged directly across from us at the other side of the ring, his leg cocked back behind him on the arena wall. Therian stood beside him, a hulking menace with a long red tongue that jutted out intermittently.

As we watched the clock tick down the minutes, a short, dark-skinned guy in a turban approached us. "Weapons check," he said by way of greeting, holding up a handheld scanner.

He ran the scanner over every inch of me, and then repeated the procedure with Eileen. "No metal objects found," he reported into his communicator. Turning to me, he instructed, "Stand by for the final countdown. The guard will direct you into the arena when it's time."

Just then, a siren blared, calling the crowd to attention. "Ladies and gentlemen, our bout is about to begin!" a voice over the stadium loudspeaker boomed out. "Please take your seats."

The guard who had escorted us into the arena and hovered nearby motioned me over to his side.

I drew in a deep breath. At least, I tried to.

I was having a hard time breathing. Or moving. Or contemplating how in the world I was going to make it through the next 30 minutes alive. Or even the next five minutes, for that matter.

Every moment since I fell in with the Resistance (had it really only been a month or so since I fell into this strange, alternate universe?) flashed before my eyes: the dying stranger on the sidewalk, the mysterious manuscript, the danger of detection by the government's spying eyes, Eileen's arrival, our escape from the androids, the descent to Subterranea, Spidus, Ginger, Lucian, Mattie Hatter's party, destabilizing, Malkin and the Queen, the Hive, Eileen's suffering at the hands of Eichmann in his torture chamber, training with Artemis, Narcissus' vision, and that solitary kiss shared with Eileen. I wanted more of those kisses.

"Fighters, take your places," the announcer boomed out.

Lucian moved into place, Therian following behind him.

This was really it.

My stomach was tied in knots. My feet refused to budge. My hands were clammy with sweat. And my mind was a blank: I couldn't remember a single tactic that had been drilled into my head over the past week.

For a moment, I wished I could start over, turn back the clock to a time when I was still clueless, still self-absorbed, still oblivious to the menace of the shadow government.

But no. That wasn't really true.

I didn't want to go back to not knowing, not caring, not engaging, turning a blind eye to pain and injustice.

I didn't want to go back to a world without Eileen.

Still... there was more at stake than my feelings for Eileen, no matter how deep they ran.

I thought back to what Narcissus had said: "You have the power to change the past, present and future if you are willing to live and die in the moment."

If I could change the past, present and future, where would I start? How far would I have to go back into the past to alter the present and the future? And what did it mean to live and die in the moment?

Something was starting to flicker at the edge of my awareness, a memory or a whisper of knowledge that remained just beyond my reach. As hard as I tried to grasp at it, it eluded me.

I thought back to my first conversations with Spidus about the manuscript and my role in the entire debacle.

"*The papers weren't delivered to me,*" I remember telling Spidus. "*I just happened to be at the wrong place at the wrong time when this guy keeled over on the sidewalk.*"

"*You think you were in the wrong place at the wrong time?*" Spidus echoed.

"*Sure,*" I shrugged. "*It was just dumb luck.*"

"*What if I told you that, in fact, you were singled out?*" Spidus asked. "*What if I told you that you were in exactly the right place at the right time, and that you were meant to get these papers, meant to trigger your P2P, meant to become an outlaw, meant to be welcomed into the fold of the Resistance?*"

"*I believe—although this is only my theory—that what you grabbed up off the street was Orwell's final warning to the future, personally delivered to you by Orwell himself. We know that Orwell ended his life in a coma,*" and endured a horrible, painful death. But we cannot rule out the possibility that Orwell may have mastered other means of communicating with the future. Time travel, perhaps."

"Time travel?" I repeated.

"Yes, time travel. Although those in a coma are in a suspended state of animation, their minds are still active and alert," Spidus said. "And the mind, as we now know, radiates outside the body and can live on even after death. What we must figure out is why he chose you, of all people, and why he chose to appear to you in this moment in time. There may be a genetic connection, which would solve the first part of the puzzle."

"Are you saying I'm related to this guy?" I asked, wide-eyed.

"Perhaps," came Spidus' reply. "Or perhaps you are a genetic messenger, of sorts. It may be that you have some form of memory stored in your DNA, just waiting for the right key to open the door. Perhaps this diary is the key."

"But why now, Spidus?" Eileen asked.

"Well, it is 2084, a century after Orwell's novel 1984 was set," Spidus ruminated, rubbing his chin. "Orwell predicted the future would resemble a boot stamping on a human face forever. It's an apt metaphor for our world today, under the dictates of the Controllers. Perhaps Orwell figured we could use a little help."

"So to sum up: you think a guy who died over a hundred years ago planted a DNA memory in me and then somehow traveled through time in order to appear on a public sidewalk in the middle of a crowded city surrounded by roboflies and gliderbots and a million government eyes in order to deliver a diary to me that will somehow unlock a vault in my mind and provide you with information that will help you to take down the Controllers?" I asked, my voice strained.

Spidus beamed. "That just about sums it up."

Eileen tugged at my arm and shook me out of my reverie. "It's time, Erik," she said as she grabbed my hand. "Whatever happens, no regrets."

I squeezed her hand in silent agreement, wishing I could say more ... do more ... "No regrets," I echoed.

CHAPTER 34
THE DANCE OF DEATH

"Kill, kill, kill."—The Crowd

We moved into position, across the ring from Lucian, Eileen standing just a few paces behind me ready to spring into action should I fall too early.

"Fighters, enter the ring," the booming voice announced.

Lucian and I stepped into the ring.

"Fighting for the government and the honor and security of our nation today is Lucian Freud," blared the loudspeaker enthusiastically. Lucian raised his fist in acknowledgment, his black eyes fixed on my face. The crowd broke into thunderous applause.

"In the opposite corner, fighting for the Resistance and attempting to overthrow the government and undermine national security, is Erik Blair," the voice proclaimed darkly. I refused to play along, standing motionless. The audience, hoping for more theatrics, booed.

"Fighters, at the sound of the first bell, you will approach each other and stand two paces apart," the announcer instructed. "At the second bell, you will have 30 minutes to vanquish your opponent. You will be allowed no weapons. There are no other rules. You will fight to the death."

The first bell sounded. Lucian, his mouth curled derisively, stepped forward. I did the same. We stood two feet apart, separated by a yawning chasm that I had no idea how to breach.

Lucian leaned forward and bared his teeth at me. "I'm going to rip your guts out and feed it to the alligator man," he snarled. His voice, magnified by some unseen technology, reverberated around the arena.

The crowd went wild.

Again, I remained silent, refusing to rise to his challenge.

The second bell sounded.

The clock began its countdown: 30 minutes to go.

Anticipating Lucian's attack, I stepped back just in time to miss his first lunge and kicked him square in the backside, sending him sprawling.

The crowd gasped.

Lucian bounded to his feet, murder in his eyes.

He charged at me, his arm raised with his index and middle finger of his right hand posed like a viper ready to rip into my skull.

The crowd, eager for blood, began chanting. "Kill, kill, kill!"

Again anticipating his attack, I raised my arm to block him and kicked out at the same time, catching him square in the chest. Once again, Lucian went down.

The clock clicked down the time: 27 minutes.

So far, I had managed to stay alive and completely on the defensive.

The crowd began to murmur. This was not the fight they had expected to see.

Enraged, Lucian crouched low, lowered his head and charged me like a battering ram. I frog leaped over him, twisting as I jumped and tangling my leg with his in order to throw him off balance.

The crowd began to cheer for me.

25 minutes to go.

For a moment, I was buoyant: I had managed to stay one step ahead of him so far.

My euphoria was short-lived.

Lucian flipped onto his back, and with a superhuman spring, propelled himself at me, slamming his booted feet into my stomach. I doubled over in pain, trying to catch my breath. The undersides of his boots were covered in sharp spikes. Incredibly, the fabric of my jumpsuit held strong and protected me from the worst of the attack.

The crowd groaned.

23 minutes to go.

Lucian followed up with a powerful wallop across my back that sent me sprawling.

20 minutes.

I had to focus on something other than the pain, or I wouldn't make it.

Sensing a movement above me, I rolled to the side, just barely escaping the underside of Lucian's spiked boot.

I crouched low, squinting through the sweat burning my eyes.

18 minutes.

I waited for Lucian's next move.

I didn't have long to wait.

With a roar like a mad lion, Lucian somersaulted into the air, scissoring his legs as he flew towards me. Gauging the distance, I rolled onto my back and kicked upwards, hitting him square in the lower back and propelling him backwards.

16 minutes.

Not wanting to give him a chance to regroup, I rushed Lucian and tackled him to the ground.

We smashed into the artificial turf.

"Fifteen minutes left in the bout," the announcer's voice rang out. "Fifteen minutes to the death."

"I'm going to rip your damn eyes from your skull," Lucian growled as he threw me off him.

Like a jackal, he sprang high in the air and prepared to pounce on me, his left hand extended, his two fingers ready to pluck my eyes from my skull.

In a blur of movement, I kicked up and out, slamming my feet against his extended hand. I heard a sickening crunch as his fingers bent backwards.

Lucian let out a roar of pain and retreated a few feet, cradling his hand, glaring at me with those black, murderous eyes.

12 minutes.

Lucian flexed his shoulders, pawed the ground and started running at me. I stood my ground.

11 minutes.

Just as he reached me and dove at me, I ducked, tossing him over my back and spun around, kicking him square in the stomach.

Now it was his turn to lie curled up in a ball, gasping for breath. I placed my foot on Lucian's throat and pressed down.

"Kill, kill, kill," the crowd chanted.

They had turned on their champion.

9 minutes.

Lucian's eyes bulged. His face turned red.

I pressed down harder.

He choked out a plea. "Erik … don't …"

I gazed down at him, this man who once was the closest thing to a brother I'd ever known.

"Love is the only force capable of transforming an enemy into a friend."

The words inscribed on the amulet Eileen had given me echoed in my mind. I eased the pressure of my foot on Lucian's throat.

8 minutes.

He took advantage of my hesitation to throw me off balance, jump on top of me and smash his fist onto my nose.

The crowd groaned.

Blood spurted out of my nose.

7 minutes.

He reached back to smash his fist into my face again and I used the opening to reach up and claw at his face, my fingers digging into his eye sockets just enough to cause pain but not blind him.

He fell backwards, screaming.

6 minutes.

"Kill, kill, kill," the crowd chanted.

Scissor kicking out, he tangled his legs with mine, so that we both were sprawled out in opposite directions, joined at the legs.

With a viselike grip, he tightened his legs and pulled me towards him. I tried to twist away, flipping us back and forth on the artificial turf.

5 minutes.

Digging his spiked heels into the turf, Lucian propelled himself upwards and over, so that he hovered just over me, a human cage about to snap shut.

He slammed his fist into the side of my head. Pain ripped through me. I saw stars.

4 minutes.

I fought not to lose consciousness, to stay in the moment.

Lucian's red-rimmed eyes glared down at me. He grabbed at my shirt and clutching it, dragged me forwards and head-butted me.

My head ricocheted backwards. I was a goner.

3 minutes.

Suddenly Lucian's eyes drifted to the right of me, to something laying on the grass. He paused, squinted and grabbed at whatever it was.

I used his momentary distraction to my advantage, throwing him off-balance and throwing my entire body weight at him.

2 minutes.

He went down with a sickening crunch, his right arm folding beneath him. I clambered out of reach and waited.

1 minute.

The crowd erupted with loud applause, yelling, "Kill him! Kill him!"

I stepped back.

The crowd grew silent.

45 seconds.

I looked up at the stunned crowd who had come to see pain, blood and death as entertainment.

"I'm not playing the game anymore," I said. My voice echoed throughout the silent stadium. "I will not trade my life for Lucian's death. I will not be a victor at his expense. I will not win if he has to lose."

O seconds.

I had beaten the clock.

The bell rang.

The crowd broke into thunderous applause.

"The time is up," the announcer boomed out. "Both fighters are still alive. But this is a fight to the death. Since Lucian is unconscious, the three-minute extension will be waived. Therefore, in keeping with the rules of this match, the audience must choose who will live and who will die. Viewers, key in your answer. You have 60 seconds on the clock to vote."

Once again, the clock counted down the seconds.

60, 59, 58…50, 40, 30, 20, 10…5, 4, 3, 2, 1.

"The time is up. The votes are in," the announcer declared. "By audience decree, the winner has been chosen. Erik Blair will live. Lucian Freud will die."

The audience went wild.

I looked in Eileen's direction, the first time since the match started that I had dared to glance her way. She stood motionless, tears streaming down her face.

If Lucian died, we would all lose.

Moving towards Lucian, I pulled him up, supporting his dead weight with my shoulder. His hand remained clenched around whatever he had snatched up off the ground. He provided no resistance.

"Erik Blair will leave the loser in the arena," the announcer blared out. "Therian the Chimera will fulfill the audience's decree."

I ignored the announcer, searching desperately for a way to get us both out of the arena alive.

Before I could manage even a few steps forward, Therian screamed and charged me, his teeth bared. I clutched Lucian close and tried to side-step the alligator man.

Bowed down with Lucian's weight and my own injuries, I was no match for him. He grabbed Lucian from me and threw him to the ground.

"Die! Die!" Therian screamed as he prepared to pounce on him.

I jumped on Therian's scaly back and held on for dear life as he attempted to buck me off.

Out of the corner of my eye, I saw a blur of movement.

One of the stormtroopers was running towards us, his laser rifle pointed at my head. Therian attempted to bow lower to give him a better shot.

As the stormtrooper got closer, I recognized him. It was the guard who had escorted us into the arena.

I continued to cling to Therian, knowing he would pounce on Lucian the moment I let go.

Just as he neared us, the stormtrooper paused, took aim and fired.

I cringed, prepared for a final blow.

Therian fell with a thud. The bullet had torn a hole in his head. Blood splattered the ground. He was dead.

The arena was in an uproar. The other stormtroopers stood gaping, motionless, unsure how to respond to this unexpected rewrite of the script.

The guard looked over at the dead Therian and unconscious Lucian. He pulled Lucian up to a standing position, nodded to me to follow, and began to lead the way out of the arena.

I wasted no time following him.

As we stepped inside the tunnel leading out of the arena, I looked around for Eileen. She had disappeared!

Stunned, I froze in place, desperately searching for any sign of her. My eyes landed on the cage with the little goat boy. It was empty, the cage door ajar.

I took a deep, calming breath.

I had to believe that Eileen was responsible for the empty cage. That she and Altair had made their escape while the arena was in chaos.

"Erik, I can't stay much longer," a voice behind me said. "You have to take Lucian and get out of here."

I knew that voice.

I looked closer at the guard.

"I know you," I said. "I've heard your voice before."

The guard nodded his head. "Yes, you know me," he said. "But we're running out of time. There will be another time to talk. For now, you must go."

"Go where?" I asked. "They've got the arena surrounded."

"Get back to the elevator that took you upstairs. Eileen will be waiting there. She has the magic bullet," he said, shifting Lucian into my arms.

"Use it to bypass the controls. The elevator can access a subterranean level. Ginger and Scar will be waiting below. They've been alerted."

"But what about you?" I asked. "When will I see you again? How do I know you?"

"You've always known me," the guard replied, lifting the visor of his helmet.

The face staring over at me had haunted me since I first saw it on the sidewalk a month earlier.

It was the man with the manuscript.

It was Orwell.

CHAPTER 35
CHASING ORWELL

"A dangerous terrorist is on the loose. Erik Blair has taken Lucian Freud hostage. Citizens are urged to take every precaution. Trust no one. Report anything suspicious. Guards will be making their way through the arena. Prepare for identification verification. Anyone who resists will be detained for further questioning."—Malkin

"Guards! Arrest those men!" It was Malkin, attempting to make his way through the crowded arena. "Call in the Atlas Fours! Do not let them get away!"

Orwell dropped his visor back in place and draped one of Lucian's arms around his neck so that we were both supporting his weight. "I'll help you get to the tunnel that leads to the elevator, but that's as far as I can go. Hurry!"

The arena and its army of stormtroopers was still reeling from all that had happened.

The announcer, clearly working off a script that didn't factor in the winner absconding with the loser with the help of a mysterious stranger, was trying to bluster his way through the pandemonium.

It wasn't working.

The crowd started chanting, louder and louder, but I couldn't make out the words. The confusion bought us a few minutes' lead time, but not much more than that.

The Atlas Fours were on the way.

Lucian was still passed out from the pain of his injuries, so at least I didn't have to worry about keeping him under control. For the moment and until we could find some way of restoring him to his former self, he was our prisoner and our enemy.

We ducked into an empty, dimly lit corridor, the same corridor Eileen and I had followed only an hour before into the arena. Everyone seemed to be in the arena.

I glanced back, squinting against the glare of the exterior lights. "Are you sure Eileen is waiting ahead?" I asked. "She didn't mention any alternate plans. When did you talk to her?"

"I didn't talk to her," Orwell huffed out, attempting to drag both me and Lucian forward. "I just know she'll be waiting for you. You're going to have to trust me on this."

"You're the one who got me into this mess in the first place," I muttered, staggering under Lucian's dead weight. "It doesn't exactly speak to your trustworthiness."

I had taken enough hits during the bout to make every step of our escape from the arena a painful one. My ribs ached. My side was on fire. And my head was throbbing.

Still, I was alive.

Lucian remained unconscious as we dragged, carried and jostled him out the side entrance. His broken arm hung uselessly at his side, the fingers still closed tightly around whatever he'd been reaching for before I tackled him.

"I know what Eileen means to you," Orwell said, his voice echoing off the concrete walls. "And I know what you mean to her. She's safe, for the moment, and she's waiting."

Somewhere, a siren started blaring. The announcer's babble was cut off mid-stream. Malkin's voice boomed out over the broadcast system.

"A state of high alert has been declared," Malkin proclaimed. "A dangerous terrorist is on the loose. Erik Blair has taken Lucian Freud hostage. Citizens are urged to take every precaution. Trust no one. Report anything suspicious. Guards will be making their way through the arena. Prepare for identification verification. Anyone who resists will be detained for further questioning."

"Take your clothes off," Orwell said, glancing around the deserted corridor. He pulled Lucian away from me and propped him up against the wall.

"Excuse me?" I said, backing up a step.

In the arena, the chanting had turned into screams and shouts. The Atlas Fours had arrived.

Orwell removed his black helmet and dropped it on the ground, unfastened the armor-plated jacket and dropped it on the helmet, stepped out of the jackboots, and shimmied out of the matching military-style pants.

His skin was pale, his body wiry and his eyes narrowed impatiently at me. He looked younger than I remembered from our first encounter. Stronger, too.

"Hurry up," he ordered. "Hand me your clothes and put these on."

Outside, the siren sounded again.

I pulled off my outer clothing, only to grab them back again. Eileen's amulet. I had placed it in a small pocket in my pants before the bout, but it wasn't there now. It must have fallen out.

"No time for that now, Blair," Orwell said, holding out his hands for my discarded clothing. "Not to worry. It will turn up."

"How...? What...?" I stammered, unnerved at his ability to seemingly read my mind and know things he should have had no way of knowing.

"I'll explain later," he said, shaking his head at me. "My time here is almost up. I won't be able to help you much longer, and you're still in great danger. You must hurry."

I snatched up the stormtrooper uniform Orwell had used to disguise himself and put it on haphazardly. It fit enough to allow me to move freely.

Orwell shrugged into my match clothes.

I did a doubletake.

I hadn't noticed much about him the first time we met, but here in the shadowed gloom beyond the arena, the resemblance was startling.

He was the same height as me. Same hair color. Even the same build, more or less. Dressed in my clothes, he looked enough like me to fool the average bystander.

"I don't understand any of this," I said. "Who are you?"

"There is a time for understanding, but this is not it," Orwell replied, placing the helmet on my head, then stepping back to examine me.

"Keep the visor down at all times," he warned. "And don't speak to anyone until you're well away from here. They've got your voice prints by now and will be scanning for any sounds you might make."

Lucian moaned, opened his eyes and looked straight at me. In a swift move, before Lucian could utter a word or sound an alarm, Orwell reached down and pressed his fingers to the side of Lucian's neck. Lucian slumped back against the wall.

"That should buy you enough time to get away from here before he wakes up again," Orwell said, pulling Lucian up and once again draping his good arm around my neck.

With Lucian between us, we staggered to the end of the corridor. Although it appeared to be deserted, it echoed with the sound of distant movements.

"Follow this corridor along the curve to the right," Orwell instructed, shifting Lucian's weight fully on me. "Once you pass the second curve, there will be a narrow hallway to the left. It will lead you back to the elevator, where Eileen should be waiting."

"What about you?" I asked. "Will I see you again?"

"You'll see me again," he said. "There is still much more to be done."

A shout sounded behind us, at the arena entrance to the corridor. We had been spotted.

"I'll head in the other direction and try to draw the guards away long enough for you to get away," Orwell said.

"But how will you get away?"

"Not to worry. I've got my own escape route," he said. "Now get moving. You need to get past that first curve and be out of sight before the search team arrives."

I nodded, took a deep breath, closed my mind to the searing pain that screamed through me each time I moved, and started down the corridor.

I stopped and glanced back.

"I still don't understand what's going on, but thank you," I said.

"Don't thank me yet," Orwell said. "The rest is up to you. They're coming."

That was the last I saw of Orwell.

The added weight of the stormtrooper uniform and the unwieldy bulk of the helmet made it even harder to move with any speed, but the shouts behind us were getting closer.

There was no going back.

As we made our way along that corridor, Lucian a dead weight at my side, my senses on high alert, the need to know that Eileen was safe and waiting for me bolstered my strength.

Step by weighted step, I dragged Lucian along until we had passed the first curve and moved out of sight.

Behind us, the shouts grew louder, the movements more frantic, then they began to recede.

The searchers had taken the bait.

They were chasing Orwell.

We reached the second curve without being discovered and then a narrow hallway, a service passageway of some kind.

The elevator was just ahead but Eileen was nowhere in sight and there was nowhere in that corridor to hide.

Every dark possibility ran through my mind: of Eileen captured, tortured, transformed.

I should never have listened to Orwell. I should have taken my chances and looked for her.

What if it was all a trick?

What if Eileen had been captured already?

What if the elevator wasn't an escape route back to Subterranea but a one-way ticket to Ghello and her gruesome hive?

I didn't know what to do.

If I went back to look for Eileen, I'd surely be captured.

If I waited much longer, I ran the risk of Lucian waking up and sounding the alarm.

Even if I accessed the elevator, I didn't have the magic bullet to bypass the controls and gain admittance to the lower levels.

Don't give up, you hear me? Fight back if you need to and if you get the chance, run.

My words to the little goat boy, Altair, came back to me. *If you get the chance, run.*

No matter how much I wanted—needed—to know that Eileen was safe, there was more at stake than just our future together. Like it or not, there was a war being fought and we were right in the thick of it.

I had to trust that somehow, in some way, there was a future waiting for Eileen and me. I had to believe that she had gotten away and was safe. I had to take this chance and get away.

There was no time to wait or look back.

I pressed the button for the elevator just as Lucian started to twitch. He was waking.

The distant sound of stomping boots and screamed orders started to grow louder. They were coming.

Lucian opened his eyes, inches away from my own, and glared over at me.

The sounds of the approaching army drew near.

The elevator dinged, signaling its arrival.

The doors slid open.

I had never seen a sight so beautiful in all my life.

"It's about time you got here," Eileen muttered, reaching out to grab Lucian's injured arm and drag us inside.

The elevator doors closed behind us just as a troop of guards began racing down the corridor. Bullets and laser guns fired at us and ricocheted off the closing doors.

Lucian's head dropped to his chest as he passed out again from the pain of having his broken arm seized so roughly, leaving me no option but to shoulder his full weight.

Altair huddled beside Eileen, clutching the magic bullet in his hands. Under her direction, he pointed it at the control panel and punched in a series of numbers.

We began the descent to Subterranea.

ACKNOWLEDGMENTS

No person is an island. The Japanese phrase *naiko no ko* ("success from inside help") is applicable to any writer of dystopian literature. Me included.

As a young man growing up in the 1950s, I was a regular theater attendee, especially the sci-fi flicks that littered the screen at the time. From the bevy of Roger Corman films to *The Creature from the Black Lagoon* to *The Invasion of the Body Snatchers* and later the films of John Carpenter, my mind was enveloped in dystopian images which have followed me the rest of my days.

When I began to read such writers as George Orwell, Philip K. Dick, Aldous Huxley and others who were, in actuality, writing about much of what they were seeing in their own times, I came to see that the future is never *there*. It is always *here* in the present with or without us, waiting to happen before our eyes. As John Lennon warned, "Living is easy with eyes closed, misunderstanding all you see."

Fiction and so-called reality are indeed one and the same. Thus, *The Erik Blair Diaries*.

I also want to credit such writers as Jim Keith, David Icke, Graham Hancock and others for stimulating much thought about so-called reality and non-reality. What are considered real and nonreal often co-join to form a more accurate perception concerning the nature of being.

As Spidus notes in *The Erik Blair Diaries*, that is a troubling subject to navigate.

Then there are those such as Nat Hentoff, Pete Seeger, Mike and Patrice Masters, Tom and Judy Neuberger, and others who encouraged me to keep trudging down the road when times got rough. That I appreciate greatly.

Thanks also to Bill Gladstone and Johanna Maaghul for agenting this book and giving its message a chance to be heard.

Finally, my admiration and gratitude goes out to my wife Nisha for her advice and editing of this manuscript. Without her love, work and support, I could not continue to do my life's work in helping maintain some semblance of freedom.

As I always say, none but ourselves can free our minds. Thus, I encourage you to read on.

—John W. Whitehead

JOHN W. WHITEHEAD is an attorney and author who has written, debated and practiced widely in the area of constitutional law, human rights and popular culture. Widely recognized as one of the nation's most vocal and involved civil liberties attorneys, Whitehead's approach to civil liberties issues has earned him numerous accolades and accomplishments, including the Hungarian Medal of Freedom and the Milner S. Ball Lifetime Achievement Award for "[his] decades of difficult and important work, as well as [his] impeccable integrity in defending civil liberties for all." As nationally syndicated columnist Nat Hentoff observed about Whitehead: "John Whitehead is not only one of the nation's most consistent and persistent civil libertarians. He is also a remarkably perceptive illustrator of our popular culture, its insights and dangers. I often believe that John Whitehead is channeling the principles of James Madison, who would be very proud of him."

Whitehead's concern for the persecuted and oppressed led him, in 1982, to establish The Rutherford Institute, a nonprofit civil liberties and human rights organization. Deeply committed to protecting the constitutional freedoms of every American and the integral human rights of all people, The Rutherford Institute has emerged as a prominent leader in the national dialogue on civil liberties and human rights and a formidable champion of the Constitution. Whitehead serves as the Institute's president and spokesperson. Whitehead has filed numerous amicus briefs before the U.S. Supreme Court, has been co-counsel in several landmark Supreme Court cases and continues to champion the freedoms enshrined in the Bill of Rights in and out of the courts. Whitehead is also a member of various groups that seek nonpartisan consensus solutions to difficult legal and constitutional issues through scholarship, activism and public education efforts.

John Whitehead is a frequent commentator on a variety of legal and cultural issues in the national media and writes a weekly opinion column, which is distributed nationwide. He has authored more than 30 books on various legal and social issues, including the best-selling *Battlefield America: The War on the American People* and the award-winning *A Government of Wolves: The Emerging American Police State*. Whitehead graduated from the University of Arkansas and the University of Arkansas School of Law. He also served as an officer in the United States Army from 1969 to 1971.

Manufactured by Amazon.ca
Bolton, ON

30032507R00120